Hello!

I was a swimmer when I was a kid. Backstroke was my specialty. (I liked it because it's easy to breathe when you're swimming on your back!) But swimming is an individual sport. I had a lot to learn about teamwork.

When you're playing on a team, you want to make sure that everyone is doing his or her best. When one teammate stumbles, the others help her up, just like in a family. Sometimes friends or teammates can seem like enemies. You might feel jealous of them or want to beat them. We all have feelings like that occasionally. The trick is to learn how to get past them.

Maggie is feeling threatened by two people in this book: a new volunteer at the clinic and a new girl on the basketball team. She has to find it in her heart to work with them both, instead of trying to drive them away.

If you ever find yourself in the same situation, I hope you'll remember how Maggie worked things out.

Laurie Halse Anderson

Collect All the Vet Volunteers Books

LAURIE HALSE ANDERSON

End of the Race

PUFFIN BOOKS
An Imprint of Penguin Group (USA) Inc.

Acknowledgments

Thanks to Norris, Jack, and Nate Chumley;
Kate A.W. Roby, D.V.M.; Joseph Nebzydoski, D.V.M.;
and Kim Michels, D.V.M.

PUFFIN BOOKS
Published by the Penguin Group
Penguin Young Readers Group, 345 Hudson Street, New York, New York 10014, U.S.A.
Penguin Group (Canada), 90 Eglinton Avenue East, Suite 700, Toronto, Ontario, Canada M4P 2Y3
(a division of Pearson Penguin Canada Inc.)
Penguin Books Ltd, 80 Strand, London WC2R 0RL, England
Penguin Ireland, 25 St Stephen's Green, Dublin 2, Ireland (a division of Penguin Books Ltd)
Penguin Group (Australia), 250 Camberwell Road, Camberwell, Victoria 3124, Australia
(a division of Pearson Australia Group Pty Ltd)
Penguin Books India Pvt Ltd, 11 Community Centre, Panchsheel Park, New Delhi - 110 017, India
Penguin Group (NZ), 67 Apollo Drive, Rosedale, Auckland 0632, New Zealand
(a division of Pearson New Zealand Ltd)
Penguin Books (South Africa) (Pty) Ltd, 24 Sturdee Avenue,
Rosebank, Johannesburg 2196, South Africa

Registered Offices: Penguin Books Ltd, 80 Strand, London WC2R 0RL, England

First published in the United States of America by Pleasant Company Publications, 2003
Published by Puffin Books, a division of Penguin Young Readers Group, 2012

1 2 3 4 5 6 7 8 9 10

Copyright © Laurie Halse Anderson 2003, 2012
Title page photo © 2011, Bob Krasner

LIBRARY OF CONGRESS CATALOGING-IN-PUBLICATION DATA
Anderson, Laurie Halse.
End of the Race / Laurie Halse Anderson.
p. cm.
Summary: After treating an injured greyhound at her grandmother's veterinary
clinic, thirteen-year-old Maggie learns about the abuse of greyhounds in the
dog-racing industry and vows to put a stop to it.
ISBN: 978-0-14-241228-2 (pb)
[1. Veterinarians—Fiction. 2. Greyhounds—Fiction. 3. Greyhound racing—Fiction.
4. Veterinary medicine—Fiction. 5. Dogs—Fiction. 6. Grandmothers—Fiction.]
I. Title
PZ7.A54385 En 2009
[Fic]—dc22 2009010304

Printed in the United States of America

To Catherine Stine, with thanks

Chapter One

. . . .

Hi, Maggie! Are you working at the clinic this afternoon? I'll walk with you." Sunita taps my shoulder as the school bus pushes us through the first heavy snowstorm of the new year.

I turn to her in the seat behind me. She's wearing a purple parka, her favorite color. "Sure," I say.

When the bus grinds to a halt, we jump off and tromp through the sparkly drifts to Dr. Mac's Place, my grandmother's veterinary clinic, where Sunita and I volunteer along with some of our friends. I live with Gran—or Dr. Mac, as everyone else calls her—in the house attached to the clinic. It's great getting to care for animals every day.

"How come you're taking the late bus?" asks Sunita. "Were you studying at the library? I didn't see you there."

"Me, at the library? You must be kidding." Even though I'm doing better in school since my science teacher, Mr. Carlson, helped me map out a study plan last year, the library is still the last place you'll find me. "I just finished basketball practice. Sunita, you should have seen it—Darla almost breathed fire when Coach Williams put me in as center. She even elbowed me when the coach wasn't looking and said I was too short to play that position. Can you believe that? I've always played center." I form a snowball, leap up, and hurl it over a branch. "Jump shot!"

"Center was Darla's regular position at her old school, right?" Sunita is more into books than basketball, but even she's heard that Darla Stone, a new girl at Ambler Middle School, considers herself the star player. I nod yes. "Proceed with caution," Sunita warns.

"Guess so," I agree. Sunita wouldn't steer me wrong. She always has the right answer.

"Who are the new patients at the clinic?"

Sunita asks. "I missed two whole weeks because of winter break."

"Ugh, don't remind me that Christmas vacation's already over." I make a face. "Let's see, there are some dogs and kittens still boarding. Gran dewormed the kittens today. They're sooo cute."

"Kitties! How many?" Sunita's a cat person. Calico, Siamese, domestic shorthair, bring them on!

"Four," I reply. "There's also a guinea pig named Podge. He has slobbers."

"Sounds awful. What's that?" asks Sunita. She tears open a bag of pretzels and offers me one.

I grab one in my gloved hand and toss it in the air. "Basket!" I catch it in my mouth, along with a bunch of snowflakes. "Slobbers is a condition where the guinea pig can't close his mouth because his teeth have grown too long. I hate to think of Podge not being able to eat properly, or even to shut his mouth."

"Can Dr. Mac trim his teeth?" Sunita asks.

"Yeah. She's scheduled to do surgery on Podge this Saturday." Only two more school days until I get to spend the day helping Gran with surgery, playing with kittens, and walking the boarder dogs. Hooray!

Sunita wraps her scarf tighter. "It sounds like a full house. Are David and Brenna around?" Our friends David Hutchinson and Brenna Lake have been volunteering at Dr. Mac's Place ever since we needed extra help shutting down an illegal puppy mill last year.

"David's around, but Brenna's family is taking an extra week in Costa Rica. They're learning about sea turtle nesting habits." Brenna's parents are wildlife rehabilitators. It's so awesome how her whole family's involved in saving endangered species.

"It would be nice to be in the tropics right about now," Sunita sighs as the snow swirls faster. We reach my front door and tap snow off our boots. Even though I'm still sweaty from practice, I shiver as a blast of wind whistles under my hood. We hurry in and close the door quickly.

"Whew, it's almost as chilly in here as it is outside." Sunita takes her coat off but pulls a sweater from her backpack.

"Gran doesn't like to heat the house when she's in the clinic all day." I flop onto the living room couch and pry off my boots, then hook my ski jacket on a peg in the closet and shiver again. It IS cold in here. My tummy's rumbling.

After basketball practice I could eat a…well, not a horse! I open the fridge. Some yogurt, left-over salad, a bunch of apples. Much too healthy. "Sunita, want some cereal?"

"No thanks, those pretzels filled me up." She opens one of Gran's veterinary magazines to an article on cat grooming.

I pour a bowl of Froot Loops and milk and gulp it down, then rinse my bowl and leave it in the sink. "Let's see if Gran needs help."

Sunita closes the magazine and follows me through the hallway door to the clinic. Friendly barks from the boarding kennels greet us.

"Gran?" I call as we step into the waiting room.

"Hello," replies an unfamiliar, high-pitched voice.

A girl sits at the receptionist desk, filing charts. Her tightly curled black hair is held back by two yellow clips, which match her sweater. The normally messy desktop has been straightened up. All the active charts and phone messages are in neat piles. She's even put the jumble of pens in a Dr. Mac's Place coffee mug!

"Who are you?" I ask. Why is she sitting at the desk, and where is Gran? Sunita's usually the one who straightens up the desk. I wonder how she feels about this.

"I'm Taryn. Taryn Barbosa. Dr. Mac asked me to help out today."

"What for?" Brenna will be back in town soon and David's right across the street. We don't need another assistant.

"Something about her granddaughter coming in late from basketball practice, and she needed someone to fill in." Dimples crease her dark cheeks.

"I'm her granddaughter, Maggie." Oh, great, joining the basketball team is suddenly a trade-off for working at the clinic?

"You look familiar, Taryn," Sunita says. "You go to Elizabeth Blackwell Elementary, don't you? Didn't you come in last year with your sick canary?"

"Yep. And I also came here last year with my sick rabbit. Dr. Mac did a great job with her. But she died this fall. She just got too old." Taryn looks sad about the rabbit but pleased that Sunita remembers her. Suddenly, I remember her, too. Taryn is the fastest runner at Blackwell, our old school. But what does she know about animals?

"Nice to meet you, Taryn," says Sunita, then

she turns to me. "I'm going to check the meds inventory in the storeroom."

"Need any help?" asks Taryn.

"Thanks, but I can handle it," Sunita replies.

Dr. Gabe, Gran's associate vet, steps out of his office. "Hey girls, how was the first day back at school?"

"Ugh," I groan. Sunita shrugs.

"That bad?" His handsome face crinkles into a grin as he pulls on his coat. "Will you tell Dr. Mac I'm off to check on that tired mama cow?"

I nod. "Sure." He helped yesterday with a tricky breech calf birth on a farm near Dr. Mac's Place. "Where's Dr. Mac?" I ask Taryn.

"She's putting the kittens back in their pen. Not only were they chock-full of roundworms, but they needed another flea bath. Yuck." Taryn gets up. "I'll go get her for you."

"That's OK." I start down the hall to help Gran when a loud vehicle rumbles up the drive. I run to the window and pull back the curtains.

An old blue truck pulls in. A woman in a faded woolen jacket jumps out, leading a badly limping dog up the steps. The doorbell jangles.

"Can I help?" Taryn beats me to the door and holds it open.

"Is this the animal clinic?" asks the woman. Her huge green eyes look frightened.

"Yes," I say, glancing at the dog. It's a bony greyhound the color of gingerbread, whimpering and shivering. "Your dog looks cold. You'd better come in, not that it's much warmer in here."

"Thanks." She stamps her snowy boots on the floor mat. "My name's Roselyn."

Gran hurries into the waiting room. "Hi, girls. Sorry, I was tied up on a phone call." Gran rubs her arms. "Brrr...That storm is really chilling everything down quickly, isn't it?"

"Snow's about a foot deep already," Roselyn says.

Gran leans over the greyhound for a better look. "Hello, what's the matter today?"

"Dog's got a bad leg," Roselyn says. She looks uncomfortable.

"I see." Gran spots the crooked bandage around the dog's leg. "Bring her right in." She motions Roselyn into the Dolittle exam room.

I can't help until I disinfect my hands, so I go to the sink and turn on the faucet. The water is cold and stays that way. It won't heat up. How could we be out of hot water? Suddenly, I realize why everyone's so cold. "Gran, the heat is off!"

"Oh, drat, I knew we should have bought a new boiler last year," Gran sighs. "Maggie, could you set out heat lamps for the kittens and the boarders?"

Sunita walks in with the meds order form on a clipboard. "Hi, Dr. Mac. We're running low on some meds."

"Sunita, glad you're here," Gran says. "Could you help Maggie with the heat lamps? Taryn, please call David Hutchinson and the boiler repairman. Sunita, show her where their numbers are on the Rolodex." As she gives orders, Gran removes the bandage and feels gently up and down the greyhound's swollen leg. The dog yelps as Gran probes with her fingers. "How long has she been like this?"

Roselyn shakes her head. "Not sure. The dog's not really mine. Maybe a week?"

Gran frowns. "I need to take some X-rays. You girls hurry with those lamps!"

I'm itching to help with the greyhound, but the lamps come first. The animals, especially the kittens, mustn't get chilled.

Chapter Two

· · · · · · · · · · ·

We'll need at least six heat lamps, two for each area," Sunita reasons. I race to check the closet.

"Here are four." I grab one in each hand.

The doorbell clangs and David Hutchinson, our volunteer from across the street, barges in. "'Scuse me, Maggie." He eyes the lamps. "Things are sure heating up in here, girls!" he cracks.

"No time for jokes, David." I check the lamps to make sure they're working.

"Dr. Mac needs you immediately in the Dolittle Room," Sunita tells him.

Sunita and I carry the lamps to the kittens' pen. The kittens are piled together to keep warm, except for one with a brown eye patch, who totters around.

"This poor baby's shivering," Sunita whispers. She puts him down next to the others. "There, little lost one, come get warm."

I place one lamp on a nearby table and the other across from it, making sure they're high enough that the kittens can't climb up, and far enough away that they won't get burned. I turn both lamps on.

We go to another bank of cages that holds a rabbit, an old gray cat, and Podge. Podge's teeth stick out from the corners of his mouth, which is matted with drool. "Don't worry, Podge, nothing a little dental wizardry can't fix." I pat him through the bars while Sunita turns on the other two lamps.

"Quick," Sunita says, "we need two more lamps for the large boarding kennels." She runs to the back storeroom while I search another supply closet. An avalanche of supplies tumbles down. What a mess. Finally, one more lamp!

"Found one," Sunita calls as she runs back.

"Me too," I reply. We enter the kennel area to a burst of barks. "Boy, it's nippy in here!"

We position the lamps at a safe distance from

the dogs. I pause by each dog to say a quickie hello. "Hey, Sparks. Hi, Goldy. You warmer now, Fletcher?" Fletcher sneezes. I pat his floppy spaniel ears. "Got to run. There's a really sick greyhound. See you later." He cocks his head and looks at me with pleading eyes. "I promise."

Sunita's still fussing with the lamps.

"C'mon, let's hurry," I say to her. "I want to get back to the greyhound."

· · · · ·

Gran gives us an update. "Just took X-rays, and the boiler repairman's on his way. David's hauled over several buckets of hot water from his house to use for scrubbing up."

The greyhound lies on the metal examining table. Her right front leg is terribly swollen, with a line of nasty, oozing cuts. David's hands steady the dog while Roselyn hovers by nervously. What are the cuts from? Did the dog fall on something?

David's in my spot. *Poor girl, I should be next to you, comforting you,* I think.

"Prepare for surgery, girls," Gran directs. "I could use your help while I clean and treat her wounds." Gran often asks us to help during surgical procedures, especially if Dr. Gabe is gone. "David, could you help Taryn cover the front desk? The boiler repairman will soon be here. Will you show him where to go?"

"Sure, Dr. Mac." David rushes off to help Taryn.

Sunita and I wash with disinfectant soap and pull on scrubs—surgical garb.

I take the dog's temperature. "Her temp is one hundred five, Gran." Normal is around one hundred one degrees.

"She has a serious fever from the infection," says Gran. She looks at Roselyn and shakes her head. "It may be too late to help her."

I know what Gran is thinking—the same thing I am. Why did this woman wait so long to get help?

Roselyn's brow creases with worry. "I thought I could heal the cuts on my own with antibiotic ointment and gauze—I didn't know it would get this bad." I feel sorry for Roselyn, but much sorrier for the dog.

Gran prepares the greyhound for an I.V. With the electric clipper, she shaves the fur from the left foreleg and from around the infected areas. Gently, I hold the dog's head down when she tries to lick her wounds. "Stay calm, now," I whisper.

Gran swabs the uninjured left foreleg with antiseptic and inserts a catheter for the I.V. "She's one sick dog. We need to treat the infection immediately and try to reduce her fever with fluids."

I stroke the greyhound's copper-colored head gently. "Hang on, girl."

"Sunita, we need an antibiotic drip," Gran says.

Sunita brings over a bag of antibiotics. Gran inserts the meds into the I.V. and hangs the bag on the I.V. pole. Next, she injects the dog with a painkiller.

The greyhound jumps and whimpers. I stroke her softly. "What's her name?" I ask.

"Gingerbread." Roselyn's face reddens as if she's on the verge of tears. "Will she make it?"

"Time will tell. Sunita, will you please show Roselyn into the waiting room? Families of the animals are generally not allowed in the room during procedures," Gran explains gently.

"I understand." Roselyn wipes her eyes on her shirtsleeve as Sunita leads her out.

Gran retrieves the X-rays and clips them onto the light box. "Hmmm...this poor girl's had quite a tumble. She has two stress fractures of the right radius. Another few centimeters and this would have been a compound fracture. That means she's broken the bone in her right front leg in two places—but not all the way through." Gran points with her pencil to the places on the film.

Sunita returns, and we all examine the film more closely. "I see it, three inches below the joint," Sunita says. "Was Gingerbread hit by a car?"

"Probably not," Gran replies. "These injuries are not typical of a car accident. They look like stress fractures—the kind of injury that comes from running very fast and falling."

I look down at Gingerbread. Her soft brown eyes gaze into mine. *Were you running? Did you fall? I wish you could tell us what happened.* She licks my hand.

Taryn pops her head in. "Dr. Mac, can I help?"

Oh, brother, she shouldn't be in here.

"Taryn, you're being a great help at the receptionist desk. Just stay there and keep answering the phone," Gran says.

"Will do, Dr. Mac," Taryn chirps on her way out.

"If it was a fall, Gingerbread really scraped herself in the process," Gran notes as she swabs out the lacerations with orange iodine antiseptic. It's a good thing Gran didn't ask for Taryn's help—Taryn would surely freak over all the pus and blood in here. Working in a veterinary clinic takes some getting used to.

"I hate to put this dog under with that fever, but those lacerations look ugly and will be very painful to clean up," says Gran. "I'll probably have to remove some dead skin. I'll wait to suture the cuts until after the infection and swelling are gone." Gran prepares an injection of creamy white liquid.

"What's that, Dr. Mac?" Sunita asks.

"It's propofol," Gran replies. "It's an ultrashort-acting anesthetic that I always use on greyhounds. They're very sensitive to anesthetics."

Slowly, Gran gives the propofol injection to relax the dog. Gingerbread's muscles go limp. I stroke her to help calm her down.

Wait a minute. This dog is way more than relaxed—her chest isn't moving at all! "Gran— she's not breathing!" My stomach twists. I can't catch my breath, either.

Gran quickly checks the color of Gingerbread's gums. "Sunita, bring the anesthetic machine and an endotracheal tube. Hurry." Sunita. runs back with the tube, and Gran slides it down the dog's windpipe. She connects it to the anesthetic machine and gives Gingerbread several breaths of oxygen.

I watch Gingerbread's chest. "She's breathing, Gran, but just barely." Tears prick my eyes. *Hang in there, Gingerbread.* I listen again. "The breaths are coming faster."

Gran exhales and shakes her head in relief. "She's pulling out of it, but this girl's too close to the edge for general anesthesia. I'll just give her a local anesthetic to numb the area around the injuries instead of completely knocking her out. Otherwise, she may not come back. Maggie, keep an eye on her vitals and inform me of any change." Gran quickly injects lidocaine near the lacerations so that she can cut and scrub without the dog feeling it.

I keep my ear close to the dog's diaphragm. *Keep breathing, Gingerbread.* "So far, so good, Gran."

"Bandage, please, Sunita," Gran requests.

Sunita offers a roll of cotton and a roll of gauze. "What about the broken bones, Dr. Mac?" she asks.

"Good question. We'll put what's called a Robert Jones bandage on her leg. It's a big, padded cotton bandage that will support the bones while we treat the wounds every day. When the infection is gone we can put on a splint or even surgically stabilize the bones." Gran wraps many layers of cotton around the greyhound's foreleg and uses the gauze to secure it in place. She listens once more to Gingerbread's heartbeat, then straightens up. "I think she's going to pull out of it, but we'll have to keep a close eye on her. Don't remove the tube until she tries to cough it out." Gran sighs deeply. "You kids are really becoming pros!" She removes her glasses, which hang on a beaded chain. "Sunita, will you help me clean up? Maggie, you can wheel the patient to the recovery room."

Before I wheel Gingerbread to recovery, I can't resist stroking her head one more time. Her ears are like velvet. One ear has a blue tattoo on the inside. I frown. Sometimes purebred dogs get a tattoo, but this one looks different, bigger. "Hey, what's this blue tattoo inside her ear, Gran? It's got some numbers and the letter B."

Gran puts her glasses back on and peers at the tattoo. "Hmmm. That's the kind of mark a racing dog gets, with her racing number, line of parentage, and age. The handlers use it to keep track of the dogs. Take her to recovery, and then let's go talk to Roselyn."

As we enter the waiting room, Roselyn looks up anxiously. "Is Gingerbread OK?" she asks. Her tired green eyes have bags under them.

"To tell the truth, it was close, but it looks like Gingerbread will pull through," replies Gran.

"What's her diagnosis?" Roselyn asks.

"Stress fractures," Gran says quietly. "They can occur if a dog is running very fast, then stumbles." Gran pauses. "Does this dog race?"

Roselyn's smile fades. "Race? I don't know anything about any racing." Is it my imagination, or does she look scared?

"Then you wouldn't know anything about a large tattoo in her ear, either?"

Gran's blue eyes can be piercing.

"The kind racing owners use to identify their dogs?" I add.

The color drains from Roselyn's pink cheeks. "No, I told you. I'd never seen that dog before last week, when some jerk pulled up in a van and dumped her right in front of my house."

Gran doesn't reply. Instead, she turns to me. "Maggie, would you please write up Roselyn's bill? I need to clean up and start my evening rounds. Don't forget homework later." I nod.

"Nice work holding down the fort," Gran says to Taryn on her way past the reception desk. "Maybe next time you can help with an animal procedure." Gran turns to me. "Oh, have you been introduced? Taryn's our new volunteer."

"We met," I answer. *You mean this is permanent?*

"I'd sure love to help with an animal next time, Dr. Mac!" Taryn looks radiant.

Taryn's much too young to be handling animals. Brenna, hurry back from Costa Rica!

As I write up the bill, I glance at the greyhound's chart. When Taryn took Roselyn's information, she wrote down the dog's name— Gingerbread—but forgot to write down Roselyn's last name or address. I'll have to mention it to Gran. After my dreaded homework's done.

Chapter Three

· · · · · · · · · · ·

There, I think everything fits," Sunita says, pushing dog-food bags and cleaning items aside to make room for the heat lamps in the supply closet.

David shoves in the last heat lamp and shuts the door before the clutter has a chance to tumble out. The heat finally came back on just as the last patient was leaving. We walk back together to the empty waiting room. David snaps his down jacket and pulls up his hood. "I'm off into the sunset on my trusty stallion."

"Make that off into knee-deep snow," I say,

opening the front door. Sunita and I laugh as David's boots sink into the drifts.

Gran picks up a stack of patient charts and groans. "I forgot about these."

"I'll file those for you," Taryn offers. "My mom's not picking me up for another ten minutes."

"Thank you, Taryn. You're a big help," Gran says.

Why does Taryn's offer annoy me so much? "Oh, Taryn," I say, picking up Gingerbread's chart and pointing to the blank lines. "Next time you need to get the owner's full name and address."

"Roselyn said she'd rather not give her last name and address." Taryn shrugs.

"That's odd," Gran remarks, then turns to me. "Maggie? Homework time." She looks at her watch. "But dinner first! There's lasagna in the fridge."

"Going right in, Gran." I turn to Sunita, wrinkling my nose. "Homework, what a time-hog."

"Don't feel bad, Maggie," Sunita sighs. "I've got a huge report on the American legislative system due in a week. I won't be able to volunteer at the clinic until the House meets the Senate on twenty pages of binder paper."

"You have to write a twenty-page essay? Yikes!" Shaking my head, I wander toward the door leading to the kitchen with my basset hound, Sherlock, at my heels.

"See ya, Maggie. It's cool getting to work with you. I saw one of your practice games last week. You were awesome on center," Taryn calls.

"Thanks," I answer halfheartedly. I don't need a cheerleader—especially not a wannabe from fifth grade.

* * * * *

My school books are spread out on the coffee table. I have a sudden urge to pick up the remote and zap on the TV to news, a silly game show, even a babyish cartoon...anything to avoid homework. But my old science teacher, Mr. Carlson, helped me set up a study guide last year, with firm rules: hardest subject first, keep moving, easier subject next, fun one last—that would be thinking up basketball strategy for tomorrow's game. Double duh!

The hardest is reading for English, so I pick up *A Tree Grows in Brooklyn*. After I spend five minutes staring at page one, with the words floating like snowflakes, the snowflake-words start to sift down into lines, and the lines settle into hard-pack sentences. The girl's story actually begins to grab me, and before I know it, I'm done with chapter one and on to my second-hardest subject: history. More reading. At least I don't have the same teacher as Sunita does, so I'm not staring a twenty-page essay in the face.

Just when I'm getting to the fun stuff (pivot-turn around my opposing point guard, bounce-pass the ball over her left knee, leaving her confused and dazed. A pass to Lucy, her pass back, ball's in my grip, pivot-turn and...BASKET!), Gran breaks my concentration.

"How's the homework coming along, Maggie?" Gran asks as she pours herself a glass of milk.

"You won't believe this, but I'm done."

"Good girl. That was fast," Gran says as she cuts herself a piece of lasagna.

I consider trying to convince Gran that my basketball practice won't prevent me from doing all my clinic chores, but I don't want to wreck this happy moment. Besides, I'm not completely sure that practice won't interfere. Instead, I ask, "Isn't Taryn a bit too new to be handling the phone?"

"We'll have to see," Gran says. "But she cleaned the kennels so fast, I didn't have anything else for her to do at that moment, and she's good on the phone. I told her to page me if she gets anything other than a routine call for an appointment." Gran's face turns serious. "That greyhound is in worse shape than I thought."

"Is she going to make it?" I stuff books back into my pack.

"If she's strong. But I may have to amputate that infected leg."

I wince at the thought. "I think I'll check on her."

"Not a bad idea. Page me if she's in trouble."

"OK, Gran." I enter the clinic and hurry down the hall. What's that noise? Is Gingerbread coughing? Maybe her lungs are collecting fluid. I open the door and turn up the light dimmers just enough to see but not enough to wake the greyhound. A patient in recovery needs her sleep. Gingerbread is hooked up to a jumble of tubes and monitors. I put my ear close to her ribs and listen to her breaths—rapid, but even. She's not coughing. The electrocardiograph shows a steady heartbeat. Gingerbread's so pretty, with her red coat and graceful torso. I hate to think of her leg coming off.

Muffled coughing sounds echo again in the hall. I approach the kennels. The cough is louder as I follow the sound to the left-hand bank of cages. It's Fletcher, the old spaniel. "Hold on, Fletcher. Easy, boy." I open his cage. He stumbles out, sneezing as I leash him. Fletcher's nose is runny and his eyes look filmy. "Let's see what we can do for you, boy." I lead him downstairs into the Dolittle Room and press the pager. "Gran, we've got a patient, but it's not Gingerbread."

• • • • •

I pull out the thermometer. "His temp is slightly elevated, Gran. It's one hundred three and a half."

"Low-grade fever." Gran examines Fletcher's floppy ears with an otoscope and listens to his lungs. "Congestion in the bronchial tubes. Read me his history, Maggie."

I open the chart. "Male cocker spaniel. Eight years old. Sinusitis at four years, acute bronchitis at six years. Bronchitis at eight years."

"Has he had all his vaccinations? Are they up to date? Be sure to check for the ones that protect against kennel cough." Gran presses up and down Fletcher's neck, but that doesn't seem to make him cough.

I scan down the list of vaccinations. "Yes, up to date. He even got the nose drops."

"Very good. We don't want kennel cough spreading like wildfire through the clinic." While I hold Fletcher, Gran swabs some mucus from his mouth and places it on a slide for viewing under the microscope. "Still, better find out what exactly is causing this cough. We'll need a chest X-ray and some blood work. Let me see that chart."

I wipe Fletcher's runny nose as Gran reads the chart.

"With this fever and congestion, Fletcher may be working on pneumonia. He's an older dog, and he may have become chilled when the heat was off. Sorry about that, Fletcher." She rubs between his ears, which sends him into doggy euphoria, a foot circling, copying the motion of her hand. "Antibiotics and a stint in the steam room will do you wonders," Gran announces. She gives him a shot of the antibiotic so fast he barely whimpers.

"What steam room, Gran?" We have a great

facility here, but since when did she install that?

"The old-fashioned kind—a steamy shower with the vaporizer on full blast!" Gran smiles. "Will you do the honors, Maggie? Get Fletcher's blanket and show him in, while I get the vaporizer."

I install Fletcher in his temporary quarters in the bathroom, on the floor near the shower stall, with the water on hot and the shower door blocked so he can't get burned. Gran puts the vaporizer up on the table so Fletcher can't burn himself on that, either. His wheezing slowly eases. He sighs and rests his head on his paws.

Once Fletcher is sleeping peacefully, I pop down the hall to take one more quick peek at Gingerbread. Her body will have to work hard to beat that nasty infection. I wonder if she'll show signs of improvement by morning. Twenty-four hours on antibiotics can make a big difference. As I turn off the lights and walk back down the hall to the kitchen door, I think about tomorrow—and my mind wanders back to basketball. Tomorrow's game against Fort Washington is an important one for our team. Will I be strug-

gling like Gingerbread? With a rush of adrena-
line, I realize that my biggest worry isn't Fort
Washington, it's Darla. Somehow, I have to stand
strong against Darla's efforts to upset me on the
court.

Chapter Four

. . . .

This morning I woke up worrying about Gingerbread. Gran said not to disturb the dog, but how can I concentrate on schoolwork, not knowing if she'll pull through? I peeked just for a sec. Gingerbread was sleeping fitfully, twisting this way and that. At least she was still alive. All through history and math I was distracted. The English class discussion of *A Tree Grows in Brooklyn* interested me, but when the last bell rang and it was time to rush into the locker room for my basketball gear, my heart started pounding, partly for Gingerbread and partly for me, getting ready to face Darla.

Now it's game time and I must force myself to focus on basketball.

"Darla on center. Maggie on power forward," Coach Williams bellows. Darla smirks triumphantly. "Lucy on small forward. Chelsea on point guard." Coach rattles on down the list, clipboard in hand, as I run to position. So Darla's back on center.

Oh, brother, is Coach Williams trying to torture me by switching us back and forth? Impossible. He's much too nice.

Fort Washington, the only team to defeat Ambler last season, nabs the ball off the jump. Their forward speeds downcourt and attempts a pass. Darla intercepts it and races to Fort Washington's basket. She leaps up and sinks a 3-point shot. Ambler cheers rise. The scoreboard clicks to Fort Washington 0, Ambler 3. Hands slap Darla high-five as she runs back to position.

"Got to be tall to sink it, Shorty!" she hisses as she passes. Maybe Darla's right. Now that I'm older and on junior varsity, everyone's sprouting up closer to that basket except me. My measly five-foot, four-inch height is starting to be a real handicap.

But Darla's not so lucky on the next go-round.

Every time she gets the ball, her block, who's hefty and all arms, has her completely covered.

Each time I'm right in there, waiting. "Pass it, Darla, I'm open!" I yell, hands waving, feet ready to bolt.

"Pass it to Maggie!" Lucy yells. She's up front as well but shadowed by a girl who blocks all escape routes. Darla scowls at me, then Lucy.

"Pass it, Darla," booms Coach Williams.

"I'm open," I yell pointlessly, realizing that Darla has no intention of passing. Ever.

Instead, she dribbles up and attempts a shot. The bullish guard intercepts the ball, charges to our basket, and smashes it in.

"Score!" roars Fort Washington's cheering section. Heavy groans rumble from the Ambler bleachers.

This pattern continues until halftime—Darla trying to shoot, even though she's blocked, while I'm wide open, shifting my legs like an impatient grasshopper. Fort Washington sinks basket after basket. Coach Williams starts to lose his cool. His face grows beet red and he paces up and down the sideline. By halftime the score is Fort Washington 18, Ambler 3.

We circle around the water jug and try to catch our breath.

"Darla," Coach Williams groans, "you've got a team here. Take advantage of it. Maggie was open many times. We know you're a good player, but even a great player can't do it all."

Darla looks mad, but she doesn't say anything.

Coach Williams makes notations in his books. "Maggie, I want you to switch with Darla. Lucy, back in on small forward."

"The coach is incompetent," Darla mutters as we jog to our spots.

"How so?" I ask, tucking in my sweaty jersey.

"He should know you're not supposed to switch the players' positions in midgame. That's amateur. The coach at my old school would never do that."

I'm tempted to blurt out that not passing to your teammates is amateur, too, but I decide it's better to keep my mouth shut and not egg her on.

The ball goes into play. I've caught it! I dribble down the court, the bullish Fort Washington guard mirroring my steps. I pivot and bounce-pass to Lucy over the guard's sturdy left knee. Lucy passes back to me, under the guard's right elbow—just as I planned. The hoop's right over me, but I don't have a chance. This guard's got me cloaked. Must try. Can't give up.

"Shoot, Maggie!" Lucy yells.

I have to prove my stuff, focus on the basket. If Gingerbread can focus every ounce of strength into recovery, so can I. *Gingerbread, this one's for you.* I toss with all my might, over the guard, and the shot sinks in. "BASKET!" The Ambler crowd jumps for joy. The score's now Fort Washington 18, Ambler 5. Just about everyone but Darla slaps me on the back. "Awesome! Way to go!"

"Great teamwork, Maggie!" Coach Williams shouts.

Darla sidles up and whispers, "Just beginner's luck, Shorty."

Yeah, right, I've only been playing this game ever since I could lift a ball!

But the next time I attempt my bounce-pass to Lucy, the Fort Washington guard steals it, races to the basket, and scores. Somehow, my touch is clumsier, slower. Somehow, the Fort Washington guard's touch is greased, totally on target. Five times the burly guard sinks it in, to resounding cheers from Fort Washington—and the next thing I know, the game's over and we've lost.

· · · · ·

"Sorry I couldn't come to cheer you on. Had to help someone in my math class," Sunita explains as we walk to the lunchroom. "How did the game go yesterday afternoon?"

I smell hamburgers and fries, normally my favorite, but I've lost my appetite since yesterday's embarrassing loss. "Not so great, Sunita. I only scored two baskets."

"Two baskets—that's wonderful!" Sunita pats my arm.

"Yeah, but I fumbled the rest. I don't know what came over me. Fort Washington smeared us." I sigh. "Maybe it had to do with Darla saying my baskets were just beginner's luck." I drop my backpack at our regular table, grab a tray, and get in line.

"Sounds like she psyched you out," Sunita replies. She chooses salad, a bag of spicy peanuts, and fruit juice.

I've managed two bites of burger and a sip of OJ when Brenna comes bounding over. *"Hola, amigas!"* She unzips her cooler and unwraps sliced green peppers, a pita sandwich with sprouts and hummus, and a carrot soda. Yuck. Way too healthy! Brenna's the only one among us who still brings her lunch to school. She claims the cafeteria food is full of hydrogenated oils, sodium nitrate, and food coloring. Whatever. I'll take school burgers and fries any day.

"I had so much fun in Costa Rica. We hung out with giant sea turtles and learned about their yearly egg-laying ritual on the beach!" Brenna grins. "I didn't miss Ambler one bit—except for Dr. Mac's Place and you guys. Fill me in, please." She takes a bite of pita and chews. Sprouts poke out of her mouth like new seedlings.

"We had quite an afternoon the day before yesterday," I start. "First of all, Gran recruited a new volunteer—Taryn Barbosa from our old elementary school. She's only in fifth grade." I roll my eyes.

"She is a bit young, but Dr. Mac says that Taryn's great on the clinic phone," Sunita says, pouring spicy nuts in her palm and crunching a mouthful. Sunita is so diplomatic.

I tell Brenna all about Gingerbread, her stress fractures and nasty cuts, how she almost stopped breathing during surgery, and what a relief it is that she's starting to pull through it all. "The weird thing was, her owner, Roselyn, wouldn't tell us where she lived or even give her last name. Roselyn seemed nervous about something, don't you think, Sunita?" She nods.

Brenna turns to say hello to Darla, who's carrying her lunch tray past our table. "Hey, Darla, come sit with us." Brenna waves her over. Darla spots me and hesitates. "Come on, Darla, don't be shy." Brenna pulls out a seat.

Darla, shy? You've got to be kidding!

Darla sits and opens her milk carton, looking uncomfortable.

"We're lab partners," Brenna explains. "Maggie, Darla, Sunita, have you all met?"

"Darla and I are both on the basketball team," I say stiffly. Darla offers a half-smile.

"Hello," Sunita says. She glances at Darla with curiosity, having heard my tale of woe.

"So go on, Maggie," Brenna urges. "Tell me more about the greyhound."

I'd rather not have Darla knowing all about Dr. Mac's Place, but Brenna's putting me on the spot, so I have no choice. "Gran said it looked like the greyhound had a racing injury. We asked Roselyn if Gingerbread was a racing dog. She got nervous again but said she had no idea."

"Greyhounds are cool," Darla says, flipping back her blond ponytail. "I have a retired racing greyhound named Hoops. He's the best dog in the whole world."

"Great," I reply halfheartedly.

"Do racing dogs make good pets?" Sunita asks. "It seems like they'd be kind of hyper."

Darla takes a gulp of milk, then continues. "They're actually very gentle, but there are certain things you have to know about retired racing dogs."

"Like what?" asks Sunita.

Darla gestures with her hands as she speaks. "They often have no experience with streets or with staying close to their owners, so until they're retrained, their owners can't let them run free. Hoops used to run off. We had to retrain him little by little."

"Hoops—cute name," Brenna chirps.

"Thanks," Darla says. "Hoops is a champ at catching passes."

"Could he sink this?" I ball up my napkin and

toss it into the nearest trash can, way over by the lunchroom door. "Score!"

Sunita and Brenna clap, but Darla's expression sours.

Sunita smiles patiently. She knows I don't act like a jerk unless I'm uncomfortable.

Riiiinngg. Saved by the bell! I jump out of my seat, never so thrilled to race off to my English class. Who knows, maybe I'll even be inspired to join the discussion of *A Tree Grows in Brooklyn.* "Catch you girls later."

Chapter Five

. . . .

On Saturday morning, Gingerbread's still feverish, but her temp's down a degree and her foreleg is less swollen. I've given her as much TLC as I can while making sure she gets tons of rest and sleep. Fletcher's been going out with me and Sherlock, my basset hound, for brief walks, bundled in a warm coat. The vaporizer and antibiotics have made his coughing fits manageable, and he's starting to act like his old self again.

There's no more snowfall, but it's absolutely freezing. All our windows have icicles and starry frost formations. There's a foot of hardpack, and if Podge's surgery wasn't scheduled for this afternoon I'd be racing down Pine Needle Hill on my sled with all the other kids in the neighborhood. All, that is, except David, who offered to shovel the walk up to the clinic. He really is a pretty good guy.

I open the clinic door to see how he's doing. A blast of cold freezes the lining of my nose. David is shoveling his way up the clinic stairs.

"Can I help?" I offer.

"Your timing is perfect. I'm almost done." He pulls his gloves off and blows on his red fingers. "Actually, you could salt it down."

"Sure. You should get inside. Looks like you're working on a case of frostbite." I open the bag of rock salt and scoop some up in an old coffee can.

"Can't. I gotta scoot. Mr. Quinn's expecting me." David puts his gloves back on and hops on his bike. He works two afternoons a week at Quinn's Stables in exchange for riding lessons. He's as crazy about horses as I am about dogs.

As I shake salt in zigzags over the icy cement steps, a gold SUV speeds up the drive. A stout woman in fur boots and a dress coat steps out, clutching a bloody towel and crying, "Emergency!" Whatever she's got in there must be in bad shape.

I hold the door open. "Come right in." I escort her toward the Herriot Room.

Gran looks up as we enter. "I'm Dr. MacKenzie. What can we do for you?"

"I'm Mrs. West," the woman says. Her voice sounds shaky, as if she's trying not to cry. "My little kitten, Missy, got attacked by my neighbor's dog. He bit her badly."

"Let's have a look." Gran helps Mrs. West lay the towel gently on the examining table and open it. We all gasp. A young kitten, once white-furred, is now red-furred. Her head leans sideways, blood pumping from a wound in her neck. Gran quickly grabs some gauze and applies pressure.

Poor kitty. Dread creeps through me.

"I had to pry that greyhound's jaws off poor Missy. It was just horrible." Mrs. West blinks back tears.

A greyhound did this? Darla said greyhounds were gentle.

Gran presses her intercom. "Taryn, would you bring me a new chart? Also, tell Brenna to prepare the recovery room and be ready for us. Maggie, prepare for surgery, please."

I scramble into scrubs and wash with antibacterial soap.

"Can you save Missy?" Mrs. West's unsteady voice cracks.

"We'll do the best we can. I'll know more after we treat her for shock and stop this bleeding. Has she had her rabies shots?" Gran asks.

"Yes. All her inoculations."

"That's good. These bites are deep. We'll leave them open and treat for infection, but the wound on her neck has a major vessel torn and some muscle damage that will need immediate attention," Gran cautions. She administers a painkiller, then cleans Missy's shoulder area and inserts an I.V. with electrolytes for shock. Next, Gran collects some blood to type it, in case Missy needs a transfusion later.

Taryn records info on the chart as I dictate: "Missy, white female cat, four months old, multiple puncture wounds, loss of blood resulting from muscle tear and lacerated vessel. Patient in shock." Taryn seems to be keeping her cool at her first sight of gore—not bad for a beginner.

"Thanks, Taryn," Gran says. "Just set the chart on the counter, then show Mrs. West to the waiting room and cover the phone."

"Sure, Dr. Mac." Taryn escorts Mrs. West out.

"Maggie, we'll need clippers, antiseptic wash,

a suture pack, and bandage material," Gran says as she hooks up Missy to the heart monitor. My own heart beats double-time. There's an awful lot of blood. I'm glad that Sunita's not here. She loves cats so much, she'd be terribly upset.

Gran shaves the kitten around all bite areas. There's the deep one on her neck and another on her back. She gently checks Missy's frail body, including her neck. "No broken bones." The kitten hardly makes a sound. I clean each injury with antiseptic and continue to apply pressure with gauze to the neck wound to reduce blood loss. As with Gingerbread, Gran decides not to put Missy under general anesthesia because she's too weak. Instead, Gran injects local anesthetic. Once the area is numb, she slowly removes the gauze and spots the pumping vessel. She uses hemostats to clamp the vessel shut.

"Now that I've stopped the bleeding," Gran says, "I can suture the torn muscle in place and then close the skin with a final layer of stitches." When Gran's finished, we clean up and bandage the wound.

"Missy has lost a significant amount of blood," Gran says. "Maggie, go find Socrates. He's the same blood type as Missy."

I run into Gran's office and find Socrates in his usual place—sitting in the middle of the desk on top of all Gran's papers. I pick him up quickly and take him to Gran. Socrates may have an attitude, but he knows when Gran means business. The swish of his tail is the only indication that he's less than happy to give blood. I hold him still while Gran draws blood from his neck with a special syringe that keeps the blood from clotting. Gran slowly administers the life-saving cells through Missy's I.V. catheter.

We watch the blips on the heart monitor, uneven and faint. Gran looks as solemn as I feel.

I whisper softly in Missy's ear. "Sweet thing, try to pull through." The kitten's ribs shudder in and out.

Gran pages Brenna to bring Missy to the recovery room. She sighs and removes her gloves. "Maggie, let's debrief Mrs. West."

In the waiting room, we explain to Mrs. West what we've done.

"Then she's going to be OK, Dr. MacKenzie?" Mrs. West looks doubtful.

"Time will tell, but there may be internal injuries we don't know about yet. Some animals

can handle major trauma like that, but others...
well, we'll hope for the best." Gran gazes at Mrs.
West. "You say your kitten was bitten by your
neighbor's greyhound?"

"Yes." She nods. "That dog came racing into
our yard and attacked Missy for no good reason. Missy must have climbed out of her box in
the garage and wandered onto the lawn. That
woman next door does not know how to con-
trol her dogs! They're always getting out of their
pens. Just last week there was still *another* dog,
whining and limping around."

"What's your neighbor's name?" I ask. Gran
shoots me a quizzical look but doesn't say anything.

"Roselyn. Roselyn Drescher." Mrs. West shakes
her head. "I don't know her very well. She keeps
to herself."

Roselyn? How many Roselyns with greyhounds could there be in Ambler? "The dog that
was limping, was it a reddish color?" I ask.

"Why yes, I think so." Mrs. West smooths the
wrinkles from her dress. "Why?"

"The dog and owner sound similar to a client
who came in here a few days ago," I reply.

Mrs. West's mouth curves downward into a frown. "If anything happens to Missy…"

Brenna bursts into the waiting room, her eyes red and teary. "Dr. Mac?"

"Yes, Brenna?" Gran turns.

"We lost Missy. Her heartbeat just stopped."

Mrs. West explodes into sobs. "My Missy!"

Each time we lose an animal, my heart breaks. I can't help picturing that little kitten in the greyhound's jaws.

"I'm so sorry, Mrs. West," Gran says gently. "We did all we could. Would you like to bring Missy's body home with you?"

Mrs. West nods, then looks at us with quiet anger. "Those dogs are dangerous. I'm going to demand that the one who killed my Missy be put to sleep, or I'll sue."

When she's finally out the door with the kitten's tiny body wrapped in a towel, I turn to Gran in the waiting room. "There are no bad dogs, only bad owners—right, Gran? Maybe that greyhound had a reason for what he did. I hear they're very gentle dogs." I can't believe I'm actually quoting Darla, as if she were some big expert. "Let's talk to Roselyn. There's something odd going on, and I want to find out what it is."

Gran nods wearily. "That's not a bad idea. I'll ask Dr. Gabe to cover, and Brenna's here, too. Taryn, can you stay a while longer? Dr. Gabe may need your help."

"You bet." Taryn beams. I swear, she's like an overeager puppy dog. Annoyance pricks at me. I go to get my coat.

Chapter Six

• • • • • • • • • • •

Isn't this Mrs. West's road?" I point to a street sign off to our right. What if it's not the same Roselyn who brought in Gingerbread? If it is, will she be angry we tracked her down? My heart skips a beat as Gran turns onto the hilly road.

"Maggie, remember, there are always two sides to a story." Gran looks over her glasses at me.

"Of course, Gran." I nod.

Gran parks in front of number 23, a smaller house than the rest, with an overgrown lawn and scrubby pines lining the porch. A whirligig twirls in the wind by the walkway. Looking closer, I see it's a wooden dog with spinning legs.

We walk up to the porch. I gather my nerve and press the bell. Dogs bark from behind the house—two or three distinct yaps. The curtain slides back an inch, a lock clicks, and the door opens. Sure enough, it is the same Roselyn—same short hair and big green eyes in a nervous face.

"Hello, Roselyn," Gran says.

Roselyn looks from Gran to me. Finally she asks, "Is Gingerbread all right, Dr. MacKenzie?"

"Gingerbread's pulling through fine," Gran answers.

I scrounge up my nerve. "Her leg is healing. But we're not here about that. I mean, not exactly." My face turns hot from embarrassment.

"May we come in?" asks Gran.

Roselyn holds open the screen door. "Please." She leads us into a small room with a few chairs and a worn sofa. "Have a seat."

A photo on the coffee table shows Roselyn with a heavy-set man in front of a stadium. Arranged along wall shelves are gold-colored trophies: greyhounds leaping in the air, greyhounds standing proudly at attention. If her dogs aren't racing dogs, then what are they—maybe show dogs? Her place hardly looks like a serious show-dog setup, but all these trophies...

Gran starts. "Your neighbor, Mrs. West, came into the clinic today with her kitten, Missy."

Roselyn squirms in her chair.

"Her kitten died!" I blurt out.

Roselyn's face stiffens. "Yes, I know. Mrs. West called me up this morning, screaming." Roselyn's knuckles turn white as she grips the armrests on her chair. "She's threatening to sue me and says she's going to have my dog, Swift, put down. Can she do that? He's a good dog, never touched an animal before. I don't know what came over him." She shakes her head from side to side. "I try to watch my dogs, but sometimes they get out." Her eyes search Gran's.

"Do you have any idea why Swift might have attacked Missy?" Gran asks.

"Not really." Roselyn's eyes shift to the floor.

"Are those statuettes along your shelves racing trophies?" I ask.

No answer. Roselyn's eyes are still focused on the rug. Why won't she look at us?

Finally, Roselyn's voice squeaks out, tight and strained. "OK, it's true. Swift and Gingerbread

and all the dogs I've owned, they're all racing dogs. Or rather, they were. Swift probably
thought he was back at the track, chasing a lure."
Roselyn looks scared, like she did at the clinic
when she first came in.

Gran exhales slowly. I can tell she's holding
back an angry response, but she speaks perfectly
calmly.

"It's not uncommon for an ex-racing dog,
who's been trained to chase a mechanical hare,
to chase small animals. Has Swift been around
any small animals outside of the track?"

"No. Well, one," Roselyn replies. "Mrs. West
has a full-grown cat, but Swift has never both-
ered it. I didn't know about the kittens until it
was too late."

"How many dogs do you have?" I ask. Gran
might be calm, but my heart is racing.

"Right now? Gingerbread, Swift, and Yellow
Bird." Roselyn's fingers loosen their grip on the
armrests. "Sometimes I have more, sometimes
less."

"Where do all the greyhounds come from?" I
ask. "There's no track around here, is there?"

"Dog racing is illegal in Pennsylvania," Gran
points out. "Roselyn, I want to make sure noth-

ing like this happens again. I'd hate to have to report you to the Humane Society."

"Please don't do that," Roselyn says nervously. "Let me explain." She hunkers down in her chair. "First of all, my name is Roselyn Drescher. My brother, Manny, and I opened Drescher's Speedway, near Bridgeport, Connecticut, about five years ago. We bought Speedway from a racing family we'd met at a dog show. It seemed like a great business at first. I love dogs, always have. I loved to watch them run. They're such graceful, beautiful creatures. Like dancers." She smiles sadly. "It was good money, lots of excitement. All our friends got into it. The business got bigger and more complex, with dog owners from all over the East Coast." She pauses. "Then…"

"Go on," Gran says softly.

"Then I began to see how the dogs were handled—like objects, or business inventory, not like animals with souls. As much as I love dogs, the business became intolerable."

"What do they do to the dogs?" I ask, not sure I want to hear the answer.

Roselyn picks at the chair fabric. "Greed does strange things to people. Not all people, mind you. Some of the owners were great. But some ran their dogs too hard, or abandoned them when they stopped winning, or even force-fed them diuretics, which remove body fluids, to make them lighter and faster, which is against gaming commission rules. And worse."

My stomach twists. "That's sickening."

"Yes," Roselyn nods. "Sickening's right. I had to get out, but I didn't tell Manny at first. I was scared of him—he has quite a temper, so I eased out slowly. When Manny realized what I was doing, he threw an absolute fit! You see, he needed my help to keep Speedway running. But, in time, he calmed down some. And I've never regretted my decision."

Roselyn pauses to gauge our reactions. I am numb, but relieved to hear the truth. Gran's brows are knit in a fierce MacKenzie scowl.

"So, how did you get Gingerbread, Swift, and Yellow Bird?" I ask.

"The last time I spoke to Manny, I asked him to bring me some of the dogs who were injured and slated to be put down. He brushed me off, but I told him that I'd report the unscrupulous handling of the dogs at his track—the diuretics, the steroids, the selling of dogs to laboratories—if he didn't agree. The gaming commission would slap him with some hefty fines, and his reputation would be muddied. So he began to send his driver down with the dogs who would die otherwise. When I get them, I try to fix them up and find them new homes."

A heaviness weighs my body down. "Why didn't you tell us that Gingerbread was an ex-racing dog from the beginning, when you first brought her in?"

Roselyn raises her hands in dismay. "I was afraid that if Manny found out I'd spilled the beans about what's going on at the track, he'd be furious—and he'd stop allowing his driver to bring me the few dogs I do get to help." She pauses, then adds, "It's been so hard to know the right thing to do. But as long as I can keep helping the dogs—" Suddenly she jumps up. "Let me introduce you to someone." Roselyn disappears into her kitchen. A screen door creaks open and shut, and a large white greyhound bounds in. He makes a beeline for me and starts wetting my hand with sloppy licks.

"Well, hello to you, too." I pet him between his pointy ears with my dry hand.

"This is Swift," Roselyn says. "He's a sweet-heart. Unfortunately, I'm afraid he's the one who ran after Missy." Swift goes to lick Gran's hand. "What will happen to him, Dr. MacKenzie? If Mrs. West sues me, can the court order Swift to be put to sleep?"

Gran responds cautiously. "She could sue for property damage, since she witnessed the attack and it occurred on her property. But she can't have Swift euthanized unless she wins a dangerous-dog suit in civil court. There's a chance Mrs. West would be satisfied without a suit if Swift was relocated."

"I see," Roselyn nods. "Dr. MacKenzie, thanks for the information. I would hate to lose Swift, but I'd rather have him relocated than dead!"

Chapter Seven

●　●　●　●　●　●　●　●　●　●　●　●

Back at the clinic, I feed and walk Gingerbread, whose temp is down to normal. She hobbles around bravely on her injured foreleg. Gran says her limp may be permanent, but at least the leg didn't have to be amputated. When we return to the kennel, Gingerbread wants me to play catch with the chew toy I couldn't resist buying for her. I tell her, "I'm beyond happy to see you rebound, but you're not quite ready for catch, Gingerbread!"

Meanwhile, Brenna has walked Fletcher and cleaned the kennels, and David has prepped the Herriot Room for Podge's procedure. After I return Gingerbread to her kennel, Brenna, David, and I lounge around the reception room, taking a breather before Podge's operation.

"It's sad to think of that sweet dog, Swift, attacking a helpless kitten," I say.

"The racing life must really traumatize the dogs," Brenna says.

"Mr. Quinn says dog racing is a much harsher business than horse racing," David adds. "He says that the dogs are basically trained to be racing machines."

I go to the front desk, switch on the computer, and grab the mouse. "Let's check online for some greyhound info."

"Good idea. It's important to back up our feelings with facts." Brenna pulls up a swivel chair beside me.

"Brenna, you sound just like your mother," David says, sitting on the desk and swinging his legs. He ducks as Brenna tries to swat him.

I scroll past all kinds of greyhound sites. Some are tracks advertising their races and dogs; some are breeders bragging about their pedigree lines; some are adoption agencies for former racing dogs, complete with photos. "You guys, listen to this," I say. "Greyhounds begin training shortly after they are born. Of the fifty thousand born each year, only twenty will generate enough money at the track to stay alive until age four!" I pause, swallowing back my anger, then continue. "It says here that the dogs are kept in cramped cages, usually measuring about three feet by three feet, until race time. After a racing injury, dogs are sometimes given painkillers and made to run before their injuries are completely healed."

"That's barbaric!" Brenna exclaims.

"And what happens to all the puppies who don't make it to the track?" David wonders.

I continue reading. "Greyhounds hit their running peak during their second and third years. When they stop winning, their owners often abandon them, have them euthanized, or send them off as lab dogs for experiments."

David shakes his head in disgust. "This whole thing makes me want to lose my lunch."

"You're not kidding," Brenna says.

Another site tells us that tracks are still legal in eighteen states, including Connecticut, where Speedway's located.

Tears cloud my eyes. "I'm so glad racing is illegal in Pennsylvania."

"The racing industry is definitely in need of some serious reform," Brenna announces sternly. She does sound just like her mom talking about issues that threaten wildlife. I can easily picture Brenna taking over her family business: Brenna on a mission to rescue river dolphins from polluted waters. Brenna telling elementary kids to cut up six-pack rings so that they don't choke seals.

"How could Manny Drescher be so uncaring that he'd sell dogs to laboratories and drop off injured dogs on someone's lawn, like he does at Roselyn's?" I ask. "We should have him arrested!"

"How would we do that?" David asks. "Besides, one of Manny's henchmen would just move up on the totem pole and keep doing the same bad stuff as before, right?"

"Yeah, that wouldn't help the dogs," Brenna points out. "We need to gather some kind of evidence—stuff that we could use to put pressure on Mr. Drescher to change his ways and treat his dogs better."

I surf the Net some more. "Guys, here's a list of activities that will get dog handlers in trouble—force them to pay fines—like messing with a dog's weight before a race. If we could go to Speedway and catch Manny's handlers doing something, maybe we could put pressure on Manny to open an adoption booth."

"Now you're talking, Maggie," Brenna says. "I'm sure that the American Greyhound Association wouldn't be too happy about some of the things that go on at Drescher's, either. We could threaten to call them and report on Manny's activities if he won't consider opening an adoption booth."

David's got the mouse now. "Hey, check this out," he says. We read over his shoulder as he scrolls through an FAQ about former racing dogs:

Do retired racing greyhounds make good pets?

Definitely! They are affectionate and patient.

Can you let your greyhound off-leash?

Not always. Greyhounds have little experience with doors other than as starting gates for races. They are so conditioned to race that when a door is opened it signals a race has begun!

Are they good with small animals?

Often they are, but sometimes they are not.

Greyhounds are trained as pups to chase the mechanical hare. They may snap at cats, hamsters, and other small animals. To combat this, they may need proper retraining.

"Retraining. That's the solution!" I shout. "Maybe Gran and I can help Roselyn find a handler for Swift. The faster he can be retrained, the faster he can find a new home far away from Mrs. West. Maybe Mrs. West would calm down and drop her threat of a suit."

"Awesome idea, Maggie," Taryn exclaims, coming into the clinic. "Maybe that trainer would also donate time to the greyhounds that'll need homes."

I guess Taryn's not that bad.

Gran walks briskly into the waiting room. "Anyone who'd like to help with Podge had better get scrubbed up. Brenna, are you staying? David?"

"I'm working at Quinn's Stables this afternoon, Dr. Mac." David glances at his watch. "Oh, man, got to go!" He throws on his parka and flies out the door.

"My mom and dad are expecting me," Brenna

replies. "We've got a wild turkey injured by a biker plus a couple of homeless owl babies."

"Sounds challenging." Gran smiles. Her dangly earrings tinkle. "I guess it's just me and my trouper, Maggie."

"Yep." I'm already climbing into my scrubs.

"I could help, too," Taryn calls eagerly. I wait for Gran to explain nicely to Taryn that she's not experienced enough for surgery.

But Gran nods. "It's about time you get some operating room know-how. This one will be a good start. It's not an emergency, so we can go slowly and I'll have time to explain procedure."

"Thanks, Dr. Mac!" Taryn's dark eyes light up with excitement.

"Maggie, get Taryn some scrubs and show her how to wash for surgery," Gran says to me with a sharp look.

Must I? Taryn follows after me, like a baby duck after her mama.

* * * * *

I steady Podge as he squirms on the metal table. The guinea pig's teeth stick out from the corners of his mouth. Poor guy, he hasn't been able to chew his food or even close his mouth for a while, so he's as bony as a stick. Gran wanted to wait a few days after his arrival to operate so she could strengthen him with glucose before this procedure.

Gran injects Podge with a sedative. "Just a little something so he won't bite us in fear when we check his mouth and file his teeth," Gran explains. The guinea pig's muscles relax and his eyes close.

"Boy, his snout sure is puffed up and red," Taryn comments.

"He has moist dermatitis from his slobbers, which we'll treat topically with an antifungal and antibiotic cream." Gran examines the inside of his mouth with a little flashlight. "First we'll need to shorten those teeth. They're too thick for the regular clipper. Maggie, will you put the burr in the dental handpiece? It's over in the drawer. Taryn, pick up that felt-tip pen. You can mark off where to cut—right about here." Gran points to show Taryn where to mark.

"What causes slobbers?" Taryn asks, screwing up her nose as she draws two lines.

"Sometimes it's hereditary—bad jaw alignment. Other times it's caused by insufficient abrasion in the diet," Gran answers. Taryn looks puzzled.

"Rodents' teeth never stop growing. They need to chew things to file their teeth down. That's one reason why beavers like to chew wood," I explain. "Podge needs some wooden blocks in his cage."

"Wow," Taryn says. "What would happen if his teeth just kept growing?"

"He wouldn't be able to eat, and eventually he'd starve to death," I tell her. Maybe this will shock Taryn enough to make her stop asking questions for a while. She nods solemnly.

I attach the dental burr, plug it in, and hand it to Gran. Then I hold Podge's jaw open while she runs the burr, a small cutting tool, back and forth over Podge's front two teeth until the extra parts fall off. After that, she smooths the surface of the teeth so they won't cut the inside of his mouth.

"Maggie, will you clean his mouth, please?"

I use antiseptic soap and gauze pads to gently clean the matted areas around Podge's mouth and apply medicated cream.

"Podge needs vitamin therapy, too," Gran says, injecting him with vitamin C. "He'll need repeated vitamin and dental treatments as well as a change of diet—more carrots and lettuce. Guinea pigs are the only mammals, aside from humans, whose bodies can't manufacture their own vitamin C. Podge will need vitamin C added to his water every day."

Taryn looks confused again. "But what does vitamin deficiency have to do with overgrown teeth?"

"Slobbers is worsened by lack of vitamin C. It creates abnormal tooth development. For example, did you notice the way Podge's teeth curved way outside of his mouth." Gran removes her gloves. "Maggie, why don't you take Podge to recovery. Taryn, you can help me clean up."

"Yes, Dr. Mac!" Taryn replies.

I've never seen someone happier to clean. I take Podge to recovery and then head off to work on a crucial piece of homework, even though it's Saturday: to psych myself into playing my best game on Monday. It's our final game against Fort Washington. I can't let my confidence be sabotaged by Darla's mind games.

Chapter Eight

• • • • • • • • • • •

The crowd is tense. I sense the energy in the gym as my knees flex nervously, anticipating the whistle. My voice is tight with tension as I call out strategy to Lucy, my small forward, and Mary, my shooting guard. Fort Washington's moms, dads, sisters, and brothers pack the bleachers to witness their team's final game. I glance at the Ambler crowd. I'm pleased to see a bunch of eighth-grade boys, including David! But our fans are outnumbered, and Fort Washington's confident cheers make it clear to everyone that they expect to win.

Coach Williams has me on center again, to

Darla's complete annoyance. She's pouting in her power forward spot. Gran waves from the crowd as the jump's about to happen. I wave back. A flicker of irritation bristles through me as I spot Taryn next to her, sharing popcorn and talking. OK, so Taryn's a clinic volunteer—but that doesn't make her Gran's best buddy

Don't go there, MacKenzie. No petty distraction. Concentrate!

Ambler gets the jump ball. Yes! Mary passes to Darla, Darla dribbles like thunder upcourt, steering way clear of Fort Washington's defense. She sinks it in, like a tossed ball in a retriever's jaw. The Ambler bleachers go wild. I have to admit, Darla's darn good when she's got a clear court. But the next time Darla gets the ball, the bullish Fort Washington guard is right on her.

The chant goes up from Mary, then Lucy, then me: "Pass it, Darla, I'm ohhh—pen!" Darla stands, stubborn. No way Darla's giving up that ball, so on her next dribble, it's intercepted by Fort Washington.

Ambler groans from the bleachers. In the crowd, I see Taryn grab her head and Gran frown. Then, miracle of miracles, Lucy intercepts Miss Bull and passes to me. I dribble up, with Lucy beside me pace for pace. There's a second guard shadowing me, an Amazon, almost six feet tall.

"Maggie!" Lucy shouts to my right.

"Hey, Shorty, pass!" Darla shouts from the basket area.

"Maggie!" Lucy repeats.

"Shorty, PASS it!" Darla screams.

Double duh, it's a no-brainer. I choose Lucy. She grabs my pass and sends it right back as we dodge past Miss Bull and Miss Amazon. All this time Darla's hogging the key area, right under the basket, hands circling, shouting, "Pass it, Shorty! What are you waiting for?"

No one calls me Shorty and gets away with it, especially not Darla. It could rain down hail, sleet, and basketballs, and I'd never pass to her. I pivot-turn, trying to decide my next move, as Miss Amazon's arms wrap around me. Before I can decide, the ref blows his whistle. He calls a time violation of the three-second rule—on me? I'm confused. No—it's on Darla, who's been camped in the key area for way too long. She turns red as a beet and stomps over as if to question the call.

After that, Fort Washington takes possession of

the ball and they hold on to it like leeches, shooting basket after basket. The Ambler fans groan. The Fort Washington crowd cheers, razzes, and generally goes haywire. Up in the bleachers Gran and Taryn look depressed. They've stopped munching popcorn and are leaning forward, elbows propped on knees. I'm embarrassed to have them witness our humbling. Mercifully, the halftime whistle blows. We spill onto the benches.

"Darla, you must give other players a chance to shoot in the key area." Coach Williams sighs. "That means you've got to get out of it and let other players circulate in. Understand?" Darla nods. He reminds her, again, to pass to her teammates. Then he lectures me about hesitating on my pass. "Whatever feud you two girls have going, leave it outside the game. We're a team, remember?" He studies his clipboard. "Alicia, center. Katie, power forward."

Hey, those are our positions.

Katie and Alicia run off. Coach Williams turns to us. "You two sit this one out and cool off." I'm mortified. How am I going to explain this to Gran? What will Taryn think of me now? Not that I care. I sneak a peek at Darla. She's frowning into her towel, wiping off sweat.

"Now who's not passing to who, Shorty?" Darla snaps.

I slide farther away from her on the bench. "I'm giving you a taste of your own medicine is all."

"You need a taste of reality," Darla snaps back. "It was you who barged into basketball, even though you're too short, and weaseled your way into my center spot."

"YOUR center spot? It was MY center spot before you ever came to this school." My hands clench into fists.

"Maggie." Coach Williams motions me over. I throw my towel on the bench.

"Maggie, you're on center. Darla on power forward. Hustle!" Coach yells, waving his hands again.

Yes! I've held on to the choice spot!

The ball is mine off the inbound pass. I dribble it up-court, leaving Fort Washington's defense in the dust. My legs feel like they're powered by jet fuel. I know it's all that spit and fire from my run-in with Darla. Whatever it is, I'm going to

use it to my full advantage! Pivot-turn, BASKET!
Ambler onlookers cheer wildly.

I catch the ball off the inbound pass. The ball
burns in my hands. Lucy and I work together:
pass, catch, pass, catch. I leap as high as Miss
Bull, grazing her hair as I sink the ball for basket
number two!

Ambler stomps the bleachers with a hundred
sneakered feet—*boom, boom, boom!* There's no
better sound in the world. The score is even
now: Fort Washington 38, Ambler 38.

"Way to go, girl!" shouts Chelsea, my point
guard.

"Dunk another, just like the other!" Lucy yells
as I sail up the court, dribbling the ball with
adrenaline-powered fury.

My thoughts flit to my canine mascot.
*C'mon, MacKenzie, all the way to victory, just like
Gingerbread!*

Just before I shoot, I glance at Gran and Taryn.
They're jumping up and down with excitement.
My own personal fans! Two cheerleaders are bet-
ter than one.

"Yaahhh!" I give a warrior's cry, leap, and
shoot. BASKET! In slow-mo, the scoreboard

clicks to Ambler 40. It's magic, pure magic—and it's my magic! Ambler fans go berserk.

There are a few more charges, up and down the court, but before I know it, the game's over and people are charging the court, dancing, singing, shouting, and slapping hands. My teammates raise me up and carry me on their shoulders. "Maa—gie, Maa—gie!"

"That's my girl!" Gran jogs onto the court, earrings jingling, and gives me a bear hug and three red roses. "I'm so proud of you."

"You were awesome," Taryn agrees, slapping me a high-five.

Gran turns to Taryn. "Taryn's quite a cheerleader. I'm hoarse from trying to keep up with her."

A hand grabs onto mine from behind. "C'mon, Maggie, Coach Williams is giving us a victory speech, then a pizza party—and you'll be the star!" Lucy shouts.

I manage to give Gran a quick hug before Lucy pulls me away. "Thanks for coming. You too, Taryn."

As I walk with Lucy toward the locker room, a sinking feeling sets in. Darla wasn't with my other teammates. She's waiting in the changing rooms, and she'll never let me forget that she wasn't the one to make those three baskets and get a victory ride on team shoulders. Torture time begins.

• • • • •

Darla corners me in the locker room after Coach Williams's speech, as I'm dressing after my shower. "You just had a lucky game today is all," she says coolly, as if she doesn't care a bit. "Oh, by the way, Brenna and I are designing a greyhound awareness poster tomorrow afternoon at her house. We're putting some up at school next week." Darla slants me a triumphant look.

I guess she's going to compete with me any way she can.

"You're not interested in helping greyhounds, Darla. You just want to horn in on my issue," I retort.

"I happen to be very interested in greyhounds," Darla says. "Remember, I'm the one who actually *has* a retired racing greyhound as a pet!" She folds her arms across her chest.

I'm so angry, my cheeks feel like they're on

fire. "Having a pet doesn't make you an expert on greyhounds," I answer. "I bet I've done lots more actual research than you." I can't believe I just said that.

"So that gives you the moral high ground?" Darla's voice has a superior edge. "As your friend Brenna says, no one owns a cause."

I don't answer, just snap my locker closed and get ready to join my teammates for a victory party. But somehow, Darla has managed to deflate my joy, like a balloon that's been stomped. If only we could take lessons from our dogs. Their minds are so pure—no head games, no revenge, no plotting and planning, just the here and now, one moment at a time. My mind shifts back to the game. Were those three awesome baskets just a lucky fluke?

Get a grip, MacKenzie!

Chapter Nine

. . . .

Early Tuesday morning I jump out of bed and
into a pair of red denims and a red-and-white-
striped T-shirt. No blue jeans allowed at Ambler,
but I can still wear my basketball sneakers.

As I'm about to burst into the kitchen, I over-
hear Gran on the telephone, making arrange-
ments for the New Tools of the Trade conference
in Connecticut this Saturday. Wait a minute—
Gran's going to Connecticut. That's where
Drescher's Speedway is! We've got to confront
Manny and put pressure on him to open an
adoption booth. Somehow I need to talk Gran
into taking me. How should I put it? *Um, I've*

always wanted to hear you talk about new veterinary tools, and oh, by the way, can we take an itty-bitty side trip to the dog track? No way that would fly. She knows I've heard her speech on veterinary tools a million times. I'll just have to ask straight out.

I gather my books—and my courage—and enter the kitchen. The aroma of coffee hits me. I love the smell but hate the taste. "Uh, Gran?"

"Morning, Maggie. You're up early," Gran says as she hangs up the phone. She pours herself some coffee.

"Well, I wanted to read through my lit notes again. We have a test on *A Tree Grows in Brooklyn* today." Not convincing. Since when have I ever studied the same notes twice before a test? Once is enough!

"That's great, Maggie—you're really working hard in school. Cereal?" Gran brings over a box of Cheerios and two bowls.

"Sure, thanks." I get the milk and pour. I'm about to pop the trip question, but she speaks first.

"I'm also proud of you for such hard work at basketball. You're really giving it your all." Gran squeezes my hand.

Soak it in, MacKenzie!

But Gran's almost as telepathic as a dog. She senses that I'm not thrilled by that last game. Her gaze is questioning. "Are you enjoying the team this year?"

Should I spill my guts? Before I can make a rational decision, my troubles explode out—all the Darla stuff, how Darla sees everything as a competition, how she hates that I've held on to my center position, how she calls me Shorty, how she won't pass to me. "I can't even feel happy about beating Fort Washington. Darla punches all the joy out of it."

Gran puts down her coffee. "Maggie, I know it's hard dealing with a bully like Darla. Bullies can say and do hurtful things. But they aren't bad people, just insecure—threatened or jealous of others. I'm not saying you should accept her behavior, but try to have a little empathy; put yourself in her shoes. She's a new girl at school and probably feels she has something to prove."

I nod. But it seems my grievances are all hooked together, sort of like the links of a choke collar, because the next thing I know, I'm asking her how long Taryn will be volunteering.

Gran searches my eyes. "Don't you think Taryn's a good addition to our team?"

"Yeah, she's pretty good, but you said you needed her because I had basketball practice and we were shorthanded. Well, Brenna's back, and basketball's almost over." I fiddle with my Cheerios, swirling them around in the milk. "Besides, isn't she a bit young? Especially when it comes to assisting with surgery."

Gran's face turns stern. "Taryn loves the work, and she's a great help. I think she's too valuable to let go just because your basketball season's coming to an end. Since Zoe left and Sunita's been so busy, the clinic is still shorthanded." Her voice softens a little. "Come on, Maggie, I know you're strong—strong enough to withstand Darla's bullying and strong enough to include Taryn." Gran gets up and puts her bowl in the sink. Then she turns around, her face slowly breaking into a smile. "You were just a little tyke when you began working at the clinic, remember? When you helped with your first surgery, you were even younger than Taryn."

"True, but I was obsessed with animals," I say.

"I think Taryn is devoted to animals, too. Don't you?" Gran asks.

"Well, she did OK with Podge, I guess."

"That's the spirit, Maggie." Gran squeezes my hand again. "Oh, by the way, I'm speaking at the New Tools of the Trade conference in Connecticut this Saturday. Would you like to stay overnight with a friend?"

Here's your chance, MacKenzie. "Can I come with you, Gran? I really want to see Drescher's track and check on the condition of the greyhounds. It's not far from the conference. I'll do all my homework in Friday study hall, and there's no practice this weekend, and—"

"Whoa, Maggie, slow down." Gran holds up her hand like a traffic guard. "A dog track is no place for a kid. Even if you are a teenager."

"Come on, Gran," I plead. "We'll be able to see Speedway firsthand. Maybe if we uncover something illegal, we can report it—or pressure Roselyn's brother to clean up his act. Brenna and David and I did research on the Internet, and we could start an adoption program right at the track, and maybe you could find a trainer who'd be willing to donate some time—"

Gran's got her hand up again. "You've got big

ideas. I'll think about it." Gran glances at her watch. "Maggie, you'd better get going. Your bus will be here any second."

It's almost impossible to change Gran's mind once it's made up, especially if it involves taking me to a place that might be dangerous. She'll never let me go to Speedway.

* * * * *

After school I walk Gingerbread for the last time. Roselyn's coming to pick her up later this afternoon.

Gingerbread is frisky and playful, catching snowballs in her mouth and sniffing the frozen drifts around the oak tree. I'm happy her foreleg is healing nicely, but I'm sad to see her go.

"Gingerbread, when Roselyn comes to pick you up, I'll ask her for advice on how to talk to her brother. If I get to go, I won't let you, Swift, and Yellow Bird down, I promise." Gingerbread licks my hand. I lead Gingerbread back to her kennel and make sure she has fresh water. Then I go into the waiting room to make a final note on her chart.

Taryn greets me, waving an Ambler basketball banner. "Will you autograph this, Maggie?"

I shrug. "OK." She hands me a pen.

Gran emerges from her office, juggling a pile of papers. "Taryn, will you get Podge, please? He needs his vitamin shot."

"I'm on it, Dr. Mac." Taryn runs off, waving the autographed banner.

Gran turns to me. "Maggie, after you file these papers, please bring Fletcher down. It's time for his antibiotic shot." I don't have the nerve to ask Gran if she's made up her mind about the track. I do tell her my idea about getting a handler for Swift so that he can find a new home faster. She thinks it's a great suggestion and says she'll call around.

The front doorbell jangles, and Brenna bursts in, whistling. Under her parka she's wearing a Screech Owl Society T-shirt, baggy rust-colored pants, and an orange bandanna tied around her long brown hair. "Hey, Maggie, guess what?" Brenna plops down in the swivel chair and spins it. Her hair flies out around her.

"What." Everyone's so cheerful—I wish I had something to be cheerful about, too.

"Remember Darla, the one on your basketball team?"

How could I forget? I nod.

"Darla wants to organize a greyhound rescue club. Great minds think alike, huh? Isn't that awesome?"

Anger rises in me like steam through a radiator. "I can't believe Darla's recruiting you for that!"

"What?" Brenna looks thoroughly confused. "I thought you'd like her idea."

"Well, here's the real deal. Darla's mad at me for supposedly stealing her position on the basketball court. Coach Williams has kept me on center, which is the position she played at her old school. So now she's just trying to copy my idea of rescuing greyhounds, just to get revenge."

"I can't believe she's that petty," Brenna says slowly.

"You'd be surprised," I snap. "What does she have in mind, anyway?"

Brenna stops swiveling. "We're meeting at school tomorrow to decide. Do you want to join us or not?"

In your dreams! Brenna doesn't get it. Darla's got Brenna under her spell.

"Work with Darla? Not a chance."

Brenna flips her long hair behind her and jumps out of the swivel chair. "There are majorly bad vibes in this room." Her tone is cold. "You're being narrow-minded, Maggie. Stop thinking about yourself for once, and think about the greyhounds. Got to do my chores." She disappears down the hall.

The clinic bell rings. I see from the window it's Roselyn. What a miserable, rotten afternoon. Brenna's mad at me, and now I've got to say good-bye to Gingerbread.

Chapter Ten

• • • • • • • • • • •

Time to go, pretty girl." I pet Gingerbread's rust-colored back and clip on her leash. "Roselyn's going to be so proud of you!" Gingerbread's nails click on the linoleum as we enter the waiting room. I dread saying good-bye.

Blasts of arctic air swirl in as the clinic door opens. "Boy, it's cold out there," Roselyn says, stamping her boots on the mat. "Hi, Maggie. Hey, Gingerbread!" Roselyn moves forward hesitantly, as if she's afraid Gingerbread has forgotten who she is.

But Gingerbread runs up and licks Roselyn's outstretched hand, her tail beating against Roselyn's worn woolen coat.

"Gingerbread's a real fighter!" Taryn says, bounding into the room. "You should have seen her playing in the snow, just as if she'd never hurt her leg at all."

Taryn, give me some space—I was going to tell Roselyn that.

Gran emerges from her office and makes post-recovery recommendations: "Don't let her run more than ten minutes at first. Make sure she doesn't get chilled. And go easy on the people food. Gingerbread must stay trim, so she doesn't have to carry much weight." Roselyn nods with each instruction. "Oh, I've spoken to a colleague of mine, Dr. Haverford. He's a master handler who specializes in greyhounds," Gran adds.

"Yes?" Roselyn's eyes light up.

"He's offered to work with Swift," Gran announces. "With his help, finding a new owner should be easier."

"That's wonderful!" Roselyn hugs Gran.

"The retraining idea was actually Maggie's," Gran adds. "And if you promise to relocate Swift, Mrs. West says she won't sue."

"Oh! Thank you so much." Roselyn hugs me,

too. "Maggie, Dr. MacKenzie, how can I repay you?" Roselyn writes a check and tears it from her checkbook. "I mean beyond this?"

"Just keep Gingerbread healthy. And don't forget to check your fences for gaps. No more great escapes!" Gran smiles. "Here's Dr. Haverford's number." Gran hands Roselyn a card, then pulls a bottle from her lab coat pocket. "Give Gingerbread a tablespoon a day of this mineral supplement to strengthen her bones."

"Thanks again." Roselyn wraps her scarf tightly and cracks open the door. Gingerbread scrambles outside, eagerly prodding her snout into snowdrifts.

"I'll help them out, Gran." I step into my boots and help Roselyn carry Gingerbread's blanket and toys. "Um, may I talk to you a minute?" I ask as Roselyn climbs into her truck.

"Sure. Hop in." She leans over to open the passenger door.

Gingerbread snuffs my shoulder as I begin. "My grandmother's giving a talk in Connecticut, not far from Bridgeport."

"Oh?" Roselyn seems surprised.

"Yes, and I'm hoping to go with her so I can visit the track, see the dogs—and try to talk your brother into opening a greyhound adoption booth."

Roselyn gets that nervous look again. "I don't think—"

I cut in. "Can you give me advice on how to talk to your brother? What do you think?" *Don't tell me I shouldn't.*

"Are you sure you want to confront Manny? He can be a little rough, and he won't take kindly to criticism." By the worried expression on her face I can tell she's underplaying her concern.

"I'm sure."

"You're braver than I am, kiddo." Roselyn shakes her head. "I'd say your best bet is to appeal to his business side—how will it make the track look good. A bit of moralizing never hurts, either. He likes to think he's playing the good guy." She grabs a pen from her handbag and a notepad from the glove compartment. She scribbles a map to Speedway, explains the route, and folds the paper into my hand. She holds it there for a moment. "Good luck, and keep me posted."

"Thanks, Roselyn." Gingerbread's curled up in a ball next to Roselyn. She must feel at home already. "Bye-bye, Ginger."

I won't let you down.

Brrring! The clinic bell jangles again, just as I'm on my way to feed and water the boarding animals. Taryn can get it. If she needs me, she can buzz me on the intercom. But suddenly a familiar voice in the waiting room stops me. The tone is high, alarmed. Where have I heard that voice before? I dash back down the hall and peer into the waiting room.

She has nerve to set foot in here!

Darla's face is all puffy and she's blubbering to Taryn. "Hoops has eaten something. He's gagging and really hyper. He needs help—quick!" Her shoulders shake as she holds Hoops in her arms.

I trudge over, feeling mad, confused, totally weird. Darla sniffs back tears and stumbles over her words. "My regular vet's on vacation. Please help me!"

Gran steps in. "What have we here?" She quickly takes in the scene and directs Darla into the Dolittle Room.

Darla's still my enemy, but this dog needs help, and fast. I help her lift Hoops onto the examining table. He's hard to steady because his feet are scratching at the metal surface in a wild scramble to jump off.

"What's wrong with him, Dr. MacKenzie? What's wrong?" Darla's almost hysterical. Hoops's black-and-white-spotted body begins to spasm violently, and his eyes roll back. We struggle to keep him from falling.

"We'll soon see." Gran pulls out her stethoscope.

"Can I help, too?" Taryn pleads. She gazes at Hoops, her brown eyes looking a little panicked.

A fifth-grader fumbling over a life-and-death matter is the last thing we need.

"You bet," Gran replies. "Bring me a new chart." Taryn rushes back to the desk.

Gran has her stethoscope on Hoops's chest. "Heartbeat's up through the roof. You say he ate something out of the norm? What was it?"

Darla has a hard time talking between sniffles. "He ate some leftover chocolates from our New Year's party."

"How many?" Gran asks.

Darla hesitates. "The whole box. About thirty pieces. I found it all torn apart on the rug," she mumbles.

"That's quite a large dose," Gran explains. "Dogs cannot metabolize theobromine, a potent chemical in chocolate." Taryn records the information on Hoops's chart.

"What can you do, Dr. MacKenzie?" Darla cries. It's so weird to see her weak and defeated like this.

"First, we need to stop Hoops from having more convulsions and slow down his heart rate. Then we'll need to get that chocolate out, before his body absorbs any more. But we need to act fast." Gran administers a shot with a mild sedative.

Hoops's muscles continue to twitch, but not as powerfully.

I grip him firmly. "Calm, boy, it's OK," I murmur.

Darla's eyes brim over as she strokes Hoops's paws.

"Maggie, why don't you show Darla out," Gran says. "Darla, I assure you that your dog is in good hands, but in an emergency we usually work without the pet's owner present," she explains gently.

I lead Darla to a seat in the waiting room. She slumps down in a chair.

Say something, I think to myself. But what? There's an awkward silence, then I leave without a word, closing the door to the Dolittle Room.

Taryn loads supplies onto a rolling cart as Gran rattles off a list: "We'll need the activated charcoal and gloves. They should be on the bottom shelf. The funnel and stomach tube should be there, too. The stomach tube is a clear, four-foot piece of tube."

"Got it," Taryn says.

"Maggie, clip a lead on Hoops and follow me." Gran leads us toward the bathroom in the grooming area.

"Once we get Hoops in the tub we'll give him an emetic," I tell Taryn.

"Emetic?" Taryn's confused.

"Something to make him barf up the chocolates," I explain.

"Barf. Oh." Taryn nods, all serious.

"It shouldn't take too long. You'll see why we do this in the tub," Gran advises.

Taryn looks like she's bracing for the worst as I hand her the leash. "Steady, Hoops," I say, gripping his torso firmly as Gran administers eyedrops.

"Is there something wrong with his eyes?" Taryn asks.

"These drops will make him nauseated," Gran

explains. "Taryn, keep a tight grip on his leash." After the drops settle in, it happens quickly. Hoops's stomach goes in, out, in under his ribs as he vomits pile after pile of chocolate.

"It's almost over, Hoops," I whisper.

"Taryn, do you want to help with the next procedure?" Gran asks. "It can be quite messy."

"No problem, Dr. Mac," she replies.

I have to admit, if Taryn's trying to prove herself, she's certainly convincing me!

Gran hands Taryn a bottle. "This is activated charcoal. Even emetics don't remove all stomach contents, so this will soak up any remaining chocolate in Hoops's tummy."

Hoops seems to have finished the last round of vomiting. He pants, exhausted. I stroke his back. "Hard work, isn't it, boy? You'll feel much better soon."

Gran smiles at me, then hands the funnel to Taryn. "You sure?"

Taryn nods. The activated charcoal looks like thick, black buttermilk.

"Taryn, I'm going to hold open Hoops's jaws and insert this tube into his stomach."

"He won't like that, will he?" Taryn asks nervously, handing me back his lead.

"No, he won't, but he'll be very happy when all is said and done," Gran replies.

"Ready," Taryn announces, her feet braced wide.

I grasp Hoops firmly while Gran opens his jaws. She slides the long stomach tube down his throat and slips a roll of tape around his upper muzzle so that he can't bite down and break the tube.

Gran turns to Taryn. "Now, once I attach the funnel to the end of the tube and hold it above his head, I want you to slowly pour in the activated charcoal."

Taryn pours, and Hoops chokes, splutters, and swallows. When the bottle is empty, Gran says, "Good work. I think he's had his fill. We'll have to repeat this in four hours and keep monitoring his theobromine levels until we're sure Hoops is out of the woods."

Gran eases the tube out of Hoops's throat. Hoops shakes his head, sneezes, and licks Taryn on the arm. I have to admit, she's been a total trouper.

Gran prepares for the next procedure. "Maggie, a bag of Ringer's, please."

I hook the electrolyte solution onto an I.V.

pole. Gran shaves a patch of fur on Hoops's fore-leg, wipes it with antiseptic, and inserts an I.V. catheter.

"What's that for?" Taryn asks, wide-eyed.

"Fluids," I explain. "Hoops has lost lots of fluid from barfing. It would be dangerous for him to get even more dehydrated. By the way, Taryn—"

She turns to me. "Yes?"

"You have a strong stomach. You really hung in there."

"I tried." Taryn laughs.

Gran smiles at us. "Maggie, let's go debrief Darla. Taryn, you can take Hoops to recovery."

In the waiting room, Darla starts out of her chair, avoiding my gaze. "Is he OK, Dr. MacKenzie?"

Gran begins the report. I pick it up in the middle. Darla finally glances at me as I finish: "We think he'll pull through, though we'll need to monitor his heart and give him one more charcoal treatment."

Darla seems completely tongue-tied but manages to mutter a quick thanks. Taryn ushers her to the front desk to get patient information while I go to the recovery room.

"You're one lucky boy," I tell Hoops. "You got here just in time." He gazes at me, panting. He's really cute, with a black spot around each eye like sunglasses. "Does Darla treat you well? I hope she treats you better than she treats other people." His long snout seems to smile. I leave him when he stretches out on his mat and begins to snore.

* * * * *

"Well, hello, Maggie." Taryn's mom, Mrs. Barbosa, greets me as she enters the clinic. Her curly black hair is pulled into a bun, and her quilted coat swishes as she shakes my hand.

"Hi. Taryn's finishing her chores," I say.

Mrs. Barbosa nods and leans an arm on one of the clinic's cluttered shelves. "You know, Maggie, Taryn thinks the world of you. She's inspired by you—your talent with the animals."

"Really?" I feel as tongue-tied as Darla was.

Mrs. Barbosa continues as Gran walks in. "You're definitely one of her role models."

This is so embarrassing. I don't deserve it. I've been pretty crummy to Taryn.

Taryn rounds the corner. "Ready, Mom. Wait

until I tell you what we did today!" She zips up her pink parka. "Bye, Dr. Mac. Bye, Maggie." Taryn and Mrs. Barbosa make their way out of the clinic.

"Come sit, Maggie." Gran leads me into her office and offers me a chair.

What now?

"You were so decent, I think you scared Darla!" Gran chuckles, then gets serious. "I'm proud of you, Maggie. You acted like a true MacKenzie today. Your mom and dad would have been proud, too."

If Gran only knew my true thoughts. "I don't think I deserve any compliments, Gran."

"Yes, you do. You were able to put your bad feelings about Darla on hold to care for her dog," she says. "And you worked as a true team with Taryn." Gran unbuttons her lab coat and removes her glasses, letting them hang on her beaded chain. She sighs, and her shoulders relax. "On another matter, I've made a few phone calls and checked whether it's OK to take kids to Speedway. I was told that families do go to watch the dogs race. Maybe I was being overprotective." She smiles. "So, I've decided to take you with me to Connecticut."

"You mean that?" Suddenly, I'm full of energy.

"On one condition."

Uh-oh.

"Taryn's mom has to visit her ailing mother in Washington, D.C., this weekend and she'd rather not take her daughter along. Mrs. Barbosa asked if Taryn could volunteer all day Saturday while she's gone, but I told her I'd be in Connecticut," Gran continues. "So I discussed the possibility of taking *both* of you girls with me—to my lecture and maybe afterward to the track."

"Really?" I shift impatiently in my chair.

"Taryn's mom thinks it's a wonderful idea." She glances at me for my reaction.

"She does?" I'm almost bouncing up and down like a little kid.

"She says Taryn's been talking nonstop about the greyhounds, your greyhound research, and your idea to open an adoption booth." Gran pauses dramatically. "Therefore, the offer stands if you're prepared to chaperone Taryn, since I'll be quite busy at the conference."

"Yes!" I jump up and give Gran an extra-tight bear hug. "YES!"

Chapter Eleven

. . . .

That speech was awesome, Dr. MacKenzie! You must be famous for inventing those veterinary tools. Comments, please?" Taryn's project for social studies is to interview people of different ages and lifestyles. She holds up the mike to her mini tape recorder, reporter-style, as Gran exits the stage after her "New Tools" keynote speech.

"Well, uh..." Gran is used to being admired and quoted, but not idolized by a fifth-grade groupie! She seems flustered, which has me giggling. "It's true that I developed a few devices, but my colleagues deserve credit, too." Gran introduces us to several veterinarians making their way down the aisle and describes their contributions to the field, which Taryn records. Gran also brags to her colleagues about us volunteering at the clinic.

When Gran goes to chat with another presenter, Taryn aims the mike at me. "Maggie MacKenzie, your thoughts on the lecture?"

My thoughts? Well, now that you ask…"I've heard Gran's speeches before, but this one was definitely the best. Her diagrams made the devices understandable, and the discussion was interesting." Studying hard in school might even be worth it, if that's what it takes to be a vet.

Taryn hands me the mike so I can interview her. "So, Taryn, what's the best thing about volunteering at Dr. Mac's Place?"

Taryn's eyes light up. "Helping sick animals, like Hoops. It was hard putting that activated charcoal down his throat, but he felt so much better afterward that it made me feel good, too."

"What were your favorite aspects of the presentation this morning?" I ask.

"It was cool to hear about the inventions, like Dr. Mac's tiny rodent toothbrush that you can set at different angles."

Gran returns. "Sorry I took so long." She directs us out of the convention center. "Ready for a bite to eat?"

"Sure," I agree, even though I'd rather skip the food and go right to Speedway. There's no doubt that Gran can read minds, because she says, "Let's just grab pizza to go, so we don't miss the afternoon races."

"So, we're going to watch a race or two and then talk to Manny, right, Gran?"

"You got it," Gran says. "Onward to pizza and Drescher's. Girls, are you ready?"

Taryn nods enthusiastically.

Am I ever!

• • • • •

Drescher's Speedway is intimidating: it's a huge indoor stadium with two restaurants, five tiers of seats, and many concession stands. The walls are lined with photos of champion greyhounds and races from earlier years.

We spot a few scattered protesters with signs that read, "Write Your Congressman to End Greyhound Racing" and "Greyhound Racing Is a Crime, Not a Spectator Sport." I'm glad to see other people are concerned about greyhounds, too.

Crowds of people fill the halls to buy refreshments and to wait in long lines trailing from a bank of windows.

"What are they waiting for?" asks Taryn.

"To place their bets," Gran says in a tight voice. I glance at the faces—a few families and tourists, and a lot of men smoking cigars. Some look worried as they examine their programs. Some are arguing.

Yuck. Cigarette and cigar smoke makes me cough. I'm not used to being in public areas that allow smoking. I feel sorry for the greyhounds, having to breathe in all that smoke while they run.

Gran quickly guides us away from the betting area. "I've never placed a bet in my life and I never will."

For all Taryn's bravado, she sticks close to Gran. She and I have gone over our plan to scout around between races, but it looks like she's thinking of chickening out. Taryn's hand rests on her tape recorder, safely nestled in the pocket of her jacket.

"Here we are, Gran." We inch along the second tier of seats, staring below at a sandy track with six cage-like glass rooms at one end. That must be the starting gate. Behind that is a row of old-fashioned scales, like the kind you weigh meat on.

"Where are the greyhounds?" Taryn asks.

"Here they come!" I point to an area behind the glass enclosures. "See the guys lifting them onto those big scales? They're weighing them."

"But why?" Taryn asks, watching as the men write the weights on a blackboard.

"All dogs in a particular race have to be the same general weight, like wrestlers," Gran explains. "Thinner dogs go faster."

"If a handler's caught using laxatives on a dog, the handler is fined," I tell Taryn. "Laxatives make the dogs lose fluids and appear lighter than they really are." She nods.

"They're putting the dogs in the starting boxes!" Taryn exclaims.

"Wow, the handlers sure push them into their boxes roughly," I add.

"I'll say," Gran says.

"The dogs are muzzled, too," Taryn notes.

Still, the greyhounds look eager. Maybe they actually like to race? In spite of myself, I feel an unexpected eagerness to see them run.

I examine my program, trying to match the

greyhounds to their names, but something's not right. "Look at your programs, guys. These dogs have such awful names! Whiskey 'n' Water, Just a Bum, Bad Girl. What kind of owners would give their pets names like that?"

"The kind of owners who think of their dogs as a business commodity, not as pets," Gran replies stiffly.

"What's that?" Taryn asks, pointing to a long rod with a dangly thing on it, rotating around the circle toward the gates.

"The track workers are setting up the mechanical rabbit," Gran explains.

"It looks like a stuffed animal," Taryn says, as the bar stops in front of the gates. She's right, it does look like a stuffed bunny, propped up forlornly on the long bar.

When the rabbit lure begins to move, the greyhounds start to howl like crazy. A buzzer sounds, the doors slide open, and six greyhounds burst onto the sandy track, each with a number sewn on a fabric piece attached to their backs by a belt. A gravelly voice blasts over the loudspeaker: "They're off!"

The greyhounds move like Olympic athletes, their muscles and joints interacting with smooth precision. I'm spellbound. They're so incredibly graceful.

Taryn jumps up and down, caught up in the excitement. "Wow! If I could run that fast, I'd beat everyone at my track meets."

"Five Dog is gaining on Three Dog," the announcer's voice blares. "Six Dog lags behind ten paces, but he's gaining, gaining on Five Dog!"

The people in the stands scream: "Go, Three Dog!" "What's the matter with you, Six Dog?" "I told you to bet on that Five Dog!"

"Why don't they call the dogs by their names?" Taryn asks.

Gran shrugs, looking disturbed.

My eyes try to keep track of each dog's progress, "They must be going about fifty miles an hour, especially Two Dog on the outside of the track."

Suddenly, as I watch, Two Dog stumbles and falls. She doesn't get up, just lies there yelping. "Oh, no!" I shout. "Let's help her." I'm ready to jump out of my seat, when a dog handler runs out.

Meanwhile, the announcer continues with his brassy play-by-play as the other greyhounds streak past the finish line. "We have an upset victory. Our frisky Five Dog, Bettor's Dream, is Drescher's winner today!" Groans and cheers rise from the stands.

The handler leads the injured greyhound out and down through what looks like a trapdoor.

"Where's he taking Two Dog—I mean, Bad Girl?" I wince as I read the name listed on the program by number two.

"I hope to an on-site vet, to get her attended to. She took quite a spill," Gran replies.

I've got to see where they've taken Two Dog. It's now or never, because the next race is in fifteen minutes. If only I could find a shred of evidence, something to use as leverage to pressure Manny into seeing that these dogs are treated better. But what? Gran will never let us snoop around in unauthorized areas. I glance meaningfully at Taryn. "Gran, I'm going to the bathroom," I announce.

"I'd better come along, Maggie. This is no place for a girl to be milling around." Gran returns her reading glasses to her shoulder bag and latches it closed.

"I'm fourteen, Gran," I sigh. "Besides, it's right

at the end of our seating area." But Gran doesn't look convinced.

Taryn jumps in, just as we'd planned. "Don't worry, Dr. Mac. I'll go, too. We'll protect each other." Taryn adopts a kung fu stance,

Gran chuckles. "OK, but come right back. I made the appointment with Manny Drescher immediately following the next race."

I give Gran a thumbs-up, and Taryn and I inch back along the row of seats. When we reach the main hall, I turn to her. "Last chance to back out. This mission might be kind of scary. And Gran will be mad at us if she finds out."

Taryn looks insulted. "My track team doesn't call me Nerves of Steel for nothing." Her sparkly brown eyes hold a dare. "How about you, Maggie—are you scared?"

"No way." *Yes way. Who are you fooling, Maggie MacKenzie?*

As we weave through the stream of people, I glance down side passages and check for doors that may lead to kennel areas. Meanwhile, Taryn's talking a mile a minute. Maybe that's her way of keeping calm. "Even my mom's grandpa, the first African American to win gold medals for the U of P's track team, couldn't run as fast as that Two Dog."

"Your great-grandfather won gold medals in track? That's awesome," I tell her—then hold up my hand. "Hear something?" Muted animal sounds reach my ears. "Do you hear a dog whining?"

"From which direction?" asks Taryn.

"Not sure." As we walk, I tilt my head at various angles, trying to pinpoint the sound. Near a metal door marked PRIVATE, the whines and whimpers get louder. "Taryn, those aren't happy sounds." I hesitate, gathering up the courage to ignore the sign and open the door.

Taryn beats me to it, flipping open the door and running down the first few steps. "C'mon, Maggie."

The dingy cellar smells of mildew, wet fur, and dog food. Rows of cages line the walls, filled with muzzled greyhounds. Some look emaciated. Some are agitated, turning round and round in their tiny spaces or clawing the sides of their cages.

"Taryn, there's Bad Girl!" The fawn greyhound is tied to a post, licking her front leg. "They haven't even bandaged her leg yet." We walk up to her slowly, and she wags her tail. I hold out my hand, and she licks it. Cautiously, I stroke the silky space between her pointed ears. "Are you hurt, Sweetie?"

"Maggie—voices!" Taryn whispers. "Let's hide." I run to join her behind a cabinet as we hear two men in conversation, coming closer.

"You've got to run in the 420 Derby on Monday. There's thousands riding on you, Bad Girl," one of the men says.

He actually expects this dog to race again so soon? I peek out. The guy leaning over Bad Girl is short and stubby. He's dressed in a derby and baggy brown khakis. The man standing over them is tall and smokes a cigar. As he exhales, I stifle an urge to cough.

Cigarro man says, "Shoot her with the pain-killer. She won't even feel that sprained ankle on Monday."

The short man takes a syringe from his pock-et, uncaps it, and injects the dog. Bad Girl yaps sharply. That is totally unethical! The Humane Society would consider this cruelty, and I know from my research that the Division of Special Revenue could slap these guys with some stiff fines. If only we had some way to prove what Manny's handlers are doing.

I glance at Taryn for her reaction. She's two steps ahead of me—she has her mini tape recorder out and is recording their conversation!

Maybe we *can* get something on Mr. Drescher— but not if they see us.

We duck down, squeezing ourselves farther behind the dusty storage cabinet as the men walk closer. Between the dust and the cigar smoke, I have to struggle not to sneeze.

"What about Whiskey 'n' Water?" a gruff voice asks. I hear the creak of a cage door and claws scratching rapid-fire against metal.

"Get this down his gullet," the other guy says. "That mongrel will never win otherwise. Weighed in too darn heavy this morning. What have you been feeding him, rocks?" Both men chortle.

More whimpering. I can't bear to hear any dog abused. Got to peek out.

The stubby man is trying to force something down the greyhound's throat while the tall man holds the dog's jaws open. Whiskey 'n' Water twists his head side to side in alarm.

I have to do something—*now*. Taryn is still tape-recording, so if the men do anything to me, at least she'll have evidence. I take a deep breath, then step out from behind the cabinet.

"What are you feeding that dog? Stop it right now!" I try to sound stern and menacing, but my legs are shaking so badly, I'm afraid I'm going to fall.

Cigarro man glares at me. "None of your business, kid. You're not allowed down here. Now scoot." His face is one bone-warping scowl.

"She said stop it!" Taryn emerges with her recording equipment. "I've got you on tape."

The stubby man startles, and the bottle falls from his hands. Taryn's actually spooked him.

I reach down and grab the bottle before he can. "It's laxative!" I shout.

The tall man throws his smoking cigar onto the floor. "Get those kids!" he yells to the stubby man.

Taryn and I run for it, with Taryn way in the lead. She is one incredible runner. We careen up the stairs, puffing and sweating, and don't stop until we are down the hall, far from that metal door. I glance back. No sign of the two creepy guys.

I pull the laxative bottle out of my pocket. "Evidence."

She pulls out her mini tape. "Evidence!"

We shake on it.

Back at the stands, we're huffing and puffing. "Girls, are you that out of shape?" Gran inquires. "Don't your coaches run you at your athletic practices?"

I can't lie to Gran—I tell her the whole story. Gran is shocked, and I know we're in for a major lecture, but all she says is, "Girls, you know what you did was potentially very dangerous. I won't go into it now. We'll talk later." Gran checks her watch. "The next race is about to begin."

I shake my head. I'm burning mad at the way those men were abusing the greyhounds. "We've seen enough, Gran," I say. "Can we meet Manny Drescher now?"

Chapter Twelve

· · · · · · · · · · ·

"Who should I tell him is here?" Manny Drescher's secretary asks, looking us up and down suspiciously. I bet she's wondering why two kids and a clean-cut suburban lady would want to chat with the likes of Manny.

"Dr. MacKenzie, Maggie MacKenzie, and Taryn Barbosa. Tell him we're friends of Roselyn's," Gran replies.

"Roselyn who?" The secretary hesitates. Is she for real, or just pretending she hasn't a clue?

"Roselyn Drescher. His sister." Gran emphasizes the last word.

"Of course." The rattled secretary regains her

composure, patting down her red hairdo. "Didn't you have an appointment for 3:00 p.m.?" Gran nods. "You're early. It's only 2:30. I'll see if he's available." She clicks off in her teetery heels and returns moments later. "Right this way."

Manny sits behind an oval desk littered with yellow and green betting forms. He's talking into a cordless phone and holds up a finger, as if to say, "Just a minute."

While he finishes his call, we look around.

Taryn nudges me. "Check out that safe, Maggie." A huge round wall safe, the kind you see in thriller movies, is embedded in the wall to the left of Manny's desk.

I point to a photo on the wall, near the safe. "Look at this." In it, a younger Manny and Roselyn stand side by side in front of Speedway, all smiles.

"From happier days," Gran notes dryly.

Manny clicks off his phone and lumbers over. He extends a hand adorned with gold rings. "Any friend of my sister's is a friend of mine.

Give me a break, Manny.

"Are you enjoying the races?" he continues. "How about that Five Dog, Bettor's Dream? Were you lucky enough to bet on a winner today?"

"I don't bet," Gran replies.

Manny continues as if he hasn't even heard her, like he's so infatuated by his voice that he wants to hear it talk, talk, talk. "I've been in this business for thirty years and I haven't seen any faster than Bettor's Dream. He's won cup after cup. Bettor will be in the American Greyhound Hall of Fame in a few years, soon as he retires." Manny grins proudly.

Taryn and I exchange glances. "What about Bad Girl, your Two Dog?" I ask, my pulse racing. "She shouldn't run again Monday after spraining her foreleg, like your men expect her to. That kind of injury takes time to heal—maybe even a couple of weeks."

"She'll do just fine." Manny's grin distorts into a downward curl. "What men?"

"We have evidence your dogs are being tampered with," Gran says. "We assume that you run a legitimate business here. But some of the dog handlers are performing unethical activities, which could get them fined and the dogs disqualified."

Manny's face twists into a scowl. He folds his

arms across his barrel chest. "We don't do anything shady here. This is a class operation, so
don't get smart with me."

"Let's keep this discussion calm, Mr. Drescher,
because I've alerted the police downstairs that I
may need their help," Gran warns. She turns to
Taryn. "Go ahead."

Taryn takes out her mini tape recorder and
clicks it to "play." The basement conversation
replays loud and clear: "Shoot her with the pain-
killer. She won't even feel that sprained ankle on
Monday." Snickers all around, then a yelp from
Bad Girl. The dog's cry hurts me, just as it did
when we heard it live.

The color drains from Manny's face. He and
his secretary stand there awkwardly.

"Forcing an injured dog to run before the
injury is healed is cruel and unethical," Gran
says, obviously shocked again by Taryn's tape
recording, but quickly regaining her composure.
"The Humane Society would like to hear about
this."

I gather my nerve to talk. "We also saw a dog
named Whiskey 'n' Water about to be force-fed
laxatives so that he'd weigh less before the next
race. Doping dogs to run before an injury is

healed and laxative abuse are both grounds to remove a dog from the active racing list. Plus there could be big fines from the Division of Special Revenue."

"My handlers don't feed their dogs any laxatives." Manny yanks his shirt farther over his belly.

"Maybe the owners are bribing the handlers—who knows?" I say. "Don't believe me? Here's the bottle." I fish into my pocket and hold it up, with the label face out. "You should be ashamed of the way your dogs are treated."

"What do you people want, anyway?" Manny shouts, pounding his fists on the table and sending a flurry of candy-colored betting forms to the floor.

Gran speaks. "We'd like to close you down. But at the very least, we want to open up a greyhound adoption booth at your track so that the older and injured dogs can find good homes instead of being abused or put to sleep."

Manny shrugs. "Listen, lady, I'm running a business, not an animal shelter. Not every dog has what it takes to be a winner. Dogs come, dogs go."

I jump back in. "But where do they go?"

"That's not my concern," says Manny. "I'm running a track here. What the owners do with their dogs is their business."

"It should be your business," Gran retorts. "You create the market for these greyhounds, so you should share the responsibility for what happens to them. Did you know that Gingerbread, one of your racers who was dropped on your sister's lawn by a Speedway van, almost died this week from infected wounds and a broken foreleg?"

"My grandmother writes a syndicated newspaper column," I point out. "She could write an exposé about Speedway and how the racing dogs are treated. Her column has millions of readers. They would be horrified to know—"

"Are you threatening me? Who do you think you are? Get out!" Manny shouts.

His secretary, glued to the spot, comes alive. "You heard him. Scram!" She points to the hallway. Manny comes at us with his fist raised. My legs are wobbly. Will I be able to run? I can hardly walk.

"May I remind you about the police downstairs?" Gran says quietly. "Shall I call them now?"

Manny doesn't answer. The veins in his fore-head bulge and pulse with anger.

I've got to try one more tack. They always say you can catch more flies with honey…"On the other hand, Mr. Drescher, if your dogs could be retrained and had safe adoptive homes to go to, we'd be so grateful. I'll bet those protesters we saw outside the track would be grateful, too, if they saw you doing good things for these dogs," I add. "We'd like to help you—"

Manny cuts me off. "An adoption booth costs money. What's in it for me?"

Gran steps in. "What's in it for you is your public image. Retraining your dogs and provid-ing them with homes after their racing days are done is just plain good business. It improves your reputation in the community. You'll get good publicity—and get rid of those pesky pro-testers downstairs. If you cooperate, I'll encour-age some of the local veterinarians to volunteer their services for the dogs to be adopted. Dog tracks should be illegal, but as long as they exist, the least we can do is see to it that the dogs are well taken care of."

Manny silently ponders our proposal.

"You know, it might not be such a bad idea, Manny," his secretary says.

"But the cost?" Manny squints suspiciously. "You people think I'm rolling in dough?"

"We'll raise the money for the adoption booth and for retraining the dogs," I explain. "We'll even staff the booth and advertise the dogs on a Web site we create and maintain. All you have to do is provide space and maybe kick in some dog food now and then."

"You won't have to spend much money on it," Taryn assures him.

"I'll think about it." Manny rakes his hands through his hair. "Good for business, huh?"

Gran smiles, but her square MacKenzie jaw juts stubbornly. "One last thing, Mr. Drescher. We'd like to take the dogs who are in the worst shape, including your Number Two dog, Bad Girl, who has no business racing again after a sprain injury."

"I'll have to call their owners. Let me see what I can do," Manny mutters.

Chapter Thirteen

· · · · · · · · · · ·

The secretary escorts us back into her office while Manny makes calls to the dog owners. After a few minutes, Manny returns.

He admits that Whiskey's owner is eager to get rid of him—Whiskey's been on a losing streak for months. Bad Girl's owners have agreed after Manny told them about the alternatives—a fine and the threat of disqualification from the gaming commission. "Like I said, I run a class operation here. No funny stuff allowed," Manny repeats. He gives us fifteen minutes to get what we need from our van and meet his driver,

Thomas Mahoney, back at Speedway's main entrance.

We quickly gather leashes and Gran's medical bag. She carries it with her wherever she goes, because she never knows when she'll get an animal emergency call on her pager.

Mr. Mahoney greets us at the entrance. He's built like a beanpole and wears a sports jacket emblazoned with Speedway's logo on one shoulder.

"So, you're friends of Miss Drescher's? She's a real nice lady, that Roselyn. Tries so hard to fix up those dogs. Got her hands full, she does." Mr. Mahoney has a soft voice with a touch of an Irish accent. I like him tons better than the two greyhound handlers, but I'm a bit nervous as he escorts us back down to the dingy basement. Will those creepy men still be there?

Gran coughs when the pungent odor of wet dog and mildew hits her sinuses. "My word, this place could use a scrub." The dogs howl and yap at our arrival.

"Here's Bad Girl," I say, kneeling beside her. She's still tied to the post and whines as I touch her foreleg. "She's licked her leg so much, it's all wet."

Gran kneels down next to me and checks the greyhound's wounded leg.

Bad Girl whimpers. I stroke her fawn-colored coat.

Gran gently places the dog's paw back on the floor. "It's a sprained carpus—wrist. We'll need to splint and bind it, but first we need to clean her up. Mr. Mahoney, is there a sink here?" asks Gran.

"Right over there." He points to a far corner, where food bowls and supplies are stacked in wobbly piles. "Vet's usually here by now, but ours had an emergency."

"I see," Gran murmurs. "Here, Taryn, fill this with warm water." Gran holds out a plastic bowl and a bottle of antiseptic soap. "You can wash her leg, very gently." Taryn nods and gets right to work. When she's done, I hold a metal splint under Bad Girl's foreleg while Gran wraps it tightly. "This will hold until we get her back to the clinic. Now, where's that other greyhound? The one that's had the laxatives?"

"Those men didn't get anything down Whiskey 'n' Water," Taryn says. "Maggie stopped them just in time."

Gran pats me on the back. "Good work,

Maggie. We'll need to check him, regardless, to make sure they haven't been feeding laxatives to him all along."

Mr. Mahoney follows me as I make my way to Whiskey 'n' Water's cage. His tail wags against the bars: *thump, thump, thump.* Mr. Mahoney opens the cage and lifts Whiskey out.

I point to his wagging tail. "Look—his tail is lopped off!"

"This one's a real wagger," Mr. Mahoney says. "He wagged his tail so much he kept hurting it. We had to cut some of it off so that it would heal."

"That's awful. These cages are much too small," Taryn says, frowning.

I gaze into Whiskey's deep brown eyes. "You're such a happy boy. Even here." But despite his wagging tail, he's trembling and panting, as if he's just run a hundred miles. "Hey, Gran, he's shaking!"

Gran comes over and listens to the dog's heart with her stethoscope.

"Is he sick, Dr. Mac?" Taryn asks anxiously.

"The heartbeat is very rapid." Gran pushes gently around his kidney area with a grim look on her face. "His kidneys have an abnormal feel.

We'd better get some fluids and electrolytes into him right away."

I gather up the portable I.V. and a container of Ringer's solution. Gran swabs an area on Whiskey's shoulder and inserts the needle. I attach the Ringer's to the needle.

"What would cause this kind of kidney problem?" Taryn asks.

"If it is laxative abuse, which I suspect from his shaky condition, the body becomes depleted of minerals, which affects the kidneys," Gran explains. "Sometimes this damage is so great, the kidneys fail." Gran's words send dread through me.

"Try not to worry, Whiskey, we'll help you." Taryn strokes his blue-grey back, which trembles violently as I insert a thermometer and Gran takes blood samples.

"His temp's below normal," I note.

"Consistent with laxative abuse," Gran remarks. "As soon as we get home, we'll get his blood results. They'll show if he's potassium depleted and how well his kidneys are functioning." She inserts the sample tubes into a plastic protector kit and packs up her medical supplies.

How could anyone mistreat an animal like this?

I clip a leash on Whiskey 'n' Water, and Taryn takes Bad Girl's leash. As we leave the raceway, both greyhounds become extremely nervous. They tremble at the clump of Mr. Mahoney's workboots along the cement and at the loud remarks of the people in the parking lot.

"Why are they so jumpy, Dr. Mac?" Taryn asks.

"They're not used to life outside the track— not cars, not open spaces, not even fresh air."

I open the van's back doors. "It's good we brought those two kennels. They'll feel more secure in them."

Gran nods. We nudge the dogs into their kennels. Whiskey shakes and Bad Girl whimpers softly.

Mr. Mahoney wishes us good luck. Taryn and I hop in back to keep an eye on the dogs. Gran drives quietly, concentrating on retracing our route back to the interstate.

The greyhounds have such sweet, innocent faces, even after all they've been through. "Taryn, I have an idea," I announce. "Let's rename the dogs. We'll pick nice names that are so close to the ones they already have that they won't even know the difference. But we will."

"Great idea, Maggie!" Taryn speaks softly to Bad Girl. "How would you like a prettier name?" Bad Girl's long snout seems upturned in a smile. "How about just plain Gal?" Bad Girl barks playfully.

"Gal?" I repeat. "That's kind of weird."

"It's not weird at all," Taryn replies. "My dad's Brazilian. Gal is a common Portuguese term for 'girl,' just as it is here, and it's a really popular girl's name in Brazil."

"Gal." I say it a few times. "It does have a cute ring to it." I gaze at Bad Girl. "Hey, Gal, you happy now?" She presses her nose to the kennel window and licks my hand. "Gal it is. Now my turn." I turn to Whiskey. "Whi, whis..." He's wagging that crimped-off tail and making a breathy sound through his open mouth. "You sound like a... whistle. That's it! Hey, Whistle, you like riding in this car?" Whistle's bandaged tail whips around the kennel like Roselyn's whirligig.

"Whistle it is," agrees Taryn.

Whoops. We forgot to ask a very important person's opinion. "Gran, what do you think of those names?"

"Whistle and Gal? Very nice." Gran smiles stiffly through the rearview mirror.

Gran seems a bit tense. I'm hoping she's so relieved that we've accomplished what we came to do that she'll spare us a lecture about our basement investigation.

But no such luck. Once we're safely pointed toward Pennsylvania and she's no longer checking the map every few minutes, Gran digs in. "Girls, I have to say, what you did—sneaking into Speedway's basement without telling me—was very dangerous." She glances from Taryn to me in the rearview mirror. "What do you have to say about that, Maggie?"

"Sorry, Gran. I should have asked you." I pause. "I was afraid you wouldn't allow it."

"Taryn?" I guess Gran isn't going to spare her. I pray Taryn won't blurt out that I put the idea in her head. I tense up, waiting for her answer.

"I'm so sorry, Dr. Mac. It was wrong of me. I got Maggie in trouble, too."

Whoa, she's taking the rap?

"If you want me to quit volunteering..." Taryn's voice cracks. Is she going to cry now?

Gran's voice is slow, determined. "Girls, I know your intentions were good and what you did was courageous. But doing the wrong thing, even for the right reason, can lead to trouble. What if those men had done something worse than simply chase you? I wouldn't have known where to look for you if you hadn't returned." She sighs. "Next time, trust me to be open-minded enough to at least consider all of your ideas."

Tears roll down Taryn's cheeks. I put my hand on hers. "C'mon, now," I whisper to her. And to Gran, I think, *Just let me get my punishment over with. And spare Taryn.*

"Maggie," Gran says, "I'd like you to write an essay on how you could have conducted your investigation in a safer way. You're smart. I'm sure you can come up with one, maybe even two, alternative scenarios."

Groan. Gran knows writing is true torture for me.

"Taryn, I can't set any punishment for you. That's your mother's domain. But she will need to know what happened—in your words—when we drop you off."

Taryn wipes her tears away and scrunches up her face, as if she's just swallowed turnips. "She'll kill me, Dr. Mac."

"I doubt she'll go that far, but you should have worried about that sooner. By the way, of course you can keep volunteering. What would we do without your good work?"

"Don't forget how helpful she is during procedures, Gran," I add, surprised at my relief that Taryn's not in trouble with Gran. Taryn beams.

Who cares about punishment? When I glance back at Gal and Whistle lying peacefully in their kennels, I feel as if I just scored ten Ambler baskets in a row.

Chapter Fourteen

· · · · · · · · · · ·

Hi, Maggie." My long-lost friend Sunita places her lunch tray next to mine. She's picked the same spicy peanuts and salad with French dressing that she always eats. I swear she's going to turn into a giant nut. "What's going on at Dr. Mac's Place? I'm finally done with my mammoth history project, so I can get back to the clinic starting tomorrow!"

"Let me guess: you got an A plus," I say, biting into a French fry.

"No, just an A." Sunita smiles sheepishly and takes a bite of salad. "I heard you and Taryn went to Connecticut, to a dog-racing track! Is that true?"

I nod. "News travels fast. Was David the messenger?" On the school bus this morning I started to tell him about it, but we got to school before I could finish. I promised to fill in details about our trip to the track at lunch.

As if on cue, David plops down in a seat next to me. "I cannot tell a lie, Maggie. I am the gossipmonger. So let's have all the gory details!" He raps his fist on the chair back for emphasis.

Brenna slides her tray next to David's. She bites into a veggie burger and takes in my story silently.

I tell them all about our detective work at Speedway, how we gathered evidence, how we almost got caught. As the story unfolds, a crowd gathers—some of the basketball team, girls from my English class, and a bunch of eighth-grade boys. I spot Darla whispering something to Brenna. Brenna clears her books off a chair so Darla can sit. My heart is pounding, partly from the excitement of retelling our saga in front of all these kids and partly from a confusing bunch of feelings because Darla's listening, too.

"Rescuing those dogs and standing up to that

sleazy racetrack owner took real nerve," one of the boys remarks.

I continue the story up to the point when we treated the dogs at Dr. Mac's Place: Gal for her sprain and Whistle for laxative abuse. "They're going to be fine. And guess who called this morning."

"Who?" David asks, hanging off his seat.

"Manny Drescher!"

"What did he want?" Sunita asks.

"He said he'd let us open an adoption booth at Speedway!" Cheers rise all around. I feel great, but the best, the absolute *best*, part is when Brenna comes up and hugs me.

"Wait until I tell my family about this," Brenna exclaims. "Maggie MacKenzie, savior of greyhounds!"

• • • • •

Brenna, David, Sunita, and I are at Dr. Mac's Place. It's almost closing time. All the kennels have been cleaned and the animals walked and fed. Gal and Whistle are getting tons of attention, playing like puppies at our feet. Sherlock is jealous, so I've put him in the living room. The track greyhounds are camped out here just until we find them homes through our new adoption program, Gingerbread's Greyhound Rescue.

We're finally working on our Web site. Sunita, our resident computer brainiac, is doing the programming. We'll have portraits of adoptive dogs and tips on keeping greyhounds as pets. We'll even have some breaking news on new legislation about dog racing, and a list of which tracks around the country have adoption services. If this project goes well, we might expand our services to other tracks. But first, we'll need lots of manpower—and money.

When Taryn arrives, we show her what we've done so far. She suggests including personality profiles for each dog, which we all think is a great idea. We're in the middle of creating our prospective owner form when the clinic bell jangles.

"I'll get it." I jump up, swing open the door, and stand there a minute, just staring.

"Hi, Maggie." Darla runs her hand through her blond ponytail. "Can I talk to you?"

You've got to be kidding. But something in Darla's face seems different. I wave her in. Gal and Whistle bound over.

"Wow! Are these the Speedway dogs?" Darla leans down to get a better look.

"Yep. C'mon, we can talk in my house next door." I don't feel like bringing Darla into our Web site workshop.

Darla follows me through the clinic and into the kitchen. Sherlock trots over and sniffs my corduroys. "I'm totally guilty of paying attention to other dogs. Sorry, boy." I pet him, show Darla to the kitchen couch, and hunker in a chair at a safe distance. "Well?"

Darla sighs and rakes her hand through her ponytail again. She must be nervous. "I don't know where to start. I just want to say, I really respect what you did at Drescher's Speedway."

Get to the point, Ball Hog.

Darla goes on. "Before I got Hoops, I read up on the greyhound racing situation. I talked to some handlers and went behind the scenes a bit, too. You're not the only one who feels outraged by it." She stares down at the carpet, not looking at me.

Your point is?

"I mean—" Darla hesitates. "What I want to say is…when I realized how much you're actually *doing* to help the greyhound cause, like going to Drescher's and mustering up the nerve to talk to the owner and confront those handlers, well—I have to admit, you really walk the walk." Darla pauses again, then looks up at me. "You know, Maggie, we aren't that different. We've actually got a lot in common."

I raise my eyes slowly, cautiously, to meet hers. She has a hopeful smile on her face. Darla's never smiled at me before, and it feels weird.

"Say something," Darla suggests.

"I'm listening" is all I can say so far.

"When I came to this school, all I had going for me was basketball," she says quietly. "Have you ever had to change schools, make all new friends?"

I shake my head no.

"Well, you're lucky. It's hard being the new girl."

Now I do have something I want to say. "Maybe, but you didn't have to be so mean to me. I never did anything to you."

"I know. I've been rude, and I'm sorry," Darla says. "I was trying to be strong. But now I see that strong is different from rude."

"I guess maybe I've been rude, too," I mumble. "The truth is, it was a real pain to have someone so good suddenly on the team, vying for my spot. I was used to being the star center." It's my turn to smile. "I have to admit, though, you're good. But you really need to *pass*."

"You're good, too," Darla says. "Your pivot-turn is awesome, for someone so short." She winks at me. "Maybe we can try working together instead of competing. Not that I won't beat you on a scrimmage." She checks my reaction.

"I'll bury the hatchet on one condition."

"What's that?"

"If you promise never again to call me Shorty."

"OK, you got it."

Suddenly, I get an idea. It's so obvious I must have been blind not to see it before. "Darla, what if we joined forces? We could use your help in running Gingerbread's Greyhound Rescue."

Darla's face lights up. "Deal, and I'll match you one," she answers.

"What do you have in mind?"

Darla leans toward me, her blue eyes sparkling. "Gingerbread's Greyhound Rescue will need money, right?"

I nod, sighing. How to get money is the one thing I haven't figured out yet.

She continues, "It'll need money for a booth, for dog handlers, for delivery expenses..."

Double duh. As if she needed to remind me how difficult this will be. "So what are you saying?"

Darla's eyes are at full-tilt twinkle. "I propose that we put on a charity basketball event. Get two teams together who will play one rip-roaring game and entertain the crowd."

My heart starts to pound with excitement. Why didn't I think of that? "That's an excellent idea, Darla! But you have to promise me one more thing."

"What's that?"

"TO PASS THE BALL!"

"Deal." Darla grins, and we shake on it.

"We're going to kick butt—and raise huge money for Gingerbread's Greyhound Rescue!" Darla shouts as she pumps her fist in the air.

Chapter Fifteen

. . . .

Darla and I put together two superstar teams, including the JVs and a handful of varsity girls of Ambler High who were sympathetic to our cause. Taryn came through with a trio of select runners from her track team. She assured us they were no ordinary fifth graders, and boy, was she right. Darla and I were opposing team captains. We named our teams after some of the dogs from Speedway: hers was the Swifts, mine was the Whistles. Brenna and Sunita plastered our school and Ambler's main streets with posters. Taryn and her teammates taped posters up at

Elizabeth Blackwell Elementary. The tickets sold like wildfire.

Coach Williams volunteered his services as ref and let us use the school gym. Darla's team won after Taryn sped past me to score the decisive basket for the Swifts. But Darla was cool and didn't rub it in. In fact, she even complimented me on my incredible pivot-basket, which I sank right under her nose. I didn't rub that in, either. I'm not sure we'll keep the niceties up one hundred percent, but we'll try for eighty-five. The game was so much fun that the Whistles and the Swifts will have a second game at Ambler's YWCA in a couple weeks.

• • • • •

It's the postgame party in our living room. All the dogs are trolling for dropped food bits. My basset hound, Sherlock, has given up trying to defend his territory and has made friends with Gal and Whistle. Socrates, our cat, is the only party pooper. He's hiding out in the bathroom behind the shower curtain.

The adults have pointy party hats on that say Gingerbread's Greyhound Rescue—and so far the kids have resisted teasing them about how silly they look! David's cracked a jillion dumb jokes but only tripped once, knocking into a bowl of chips, which the dogs "vacuumed" right up for him.

I greet Roselyn and Gingerbread, who looks sleek and healthy and walks with only the slightest limp. "Mrs. West called to wish us well and to thank us for relocating Swift," I tell her. Until we find him a new home, Swift has been staying with Gran's friend Dr. Haverford, who's retraining him.

Dr. Haverford joins in the conversation. "Swift is a very smart dog. He's already getting used to my cat, and he's responding well to training."

"That's wonderful news," Roselyn says.

Some of the eighth-grade boys, our game's loudest cheerleaders, have shown up, mainly for the feast. "What's this?" asks one of them, examining a platter of food.

Sunita answers. "It's an Indian dish my mom made called *masala murgh*—it's really glorified roast chicken."

"Yum, chicken," the boy says, digging in.

"Try my dad's concoction," Taryn suggests.

"It's a spicy dish from Brazil called *feijoada*—pork and bean stew." The boys load up their plates with stew as well.

"Don't forget my mom's cookies," David adds, pointing to a batch of cookies decorated like basketballs. I don't see how the boys can add one more thing to their plates, but they manage to pile on a few cookies each. I eat one, too. Darla sidles up to the table and picks up two slices of take-out pizza, the ones Gran and I had delivered. Well, not everyone can be a gourmet cook!

After we all eat, I go up in front of the room and try to shush the crowd. "I want to take this moment to thank everyone who came out to support our effort today," I begin. People stop chatting and turn to listen. "Between ticket sales and contributions, we've raised over a thousand dollars for Gingerbread's Greyhound Rescue!" Rousing cheers fill the living room. I continue. "Soon there will be greyhounds available through our adoption Web site—great dogs like Whistle and Gal, who are running around somewhere in my house as we speak. We're lucky to have the services of Dr. Haverford, a colleague of Dr. Mac's." I point to him, and he waves his hand at the crowd. "He's already retrained one of the dogs, Swift, who's just been placed with a new owner in Maple Glen. He's donating his time to retrain more of Speedway's retired dogs so that they'll be well-adapted to the outside world before they move in with their new owners." Everyone claps.

Taryn comes over with Gal, whose tawny fur looks gorgeous after a bath and brushing. "I'd like to announce that I'm about to adopt a Speedway dog," Taryn states. "I am the proud new owner of Gal!" More hearty claps. "Finally, a pet who can go on morning runs with Mom and me." Everyone smiles. Mrs. Barbosa gazes proudly at her daughter.

I round up Whistle, who looks great in his new purple collar. He's sharing a flattened pig-in-a-blanket with Sherlock. "We happen to have another handsome greyhound from Gingerbread's Greyhound Rescue with us today. Meet Whistle." Oohs and aahs ripple through the room. "If there are any prospective owners out there, please raise your hands."

Coach Williams's hand shoots up. He steps to the mike. "I've been looking for an athletic pet to keep me company. What do you think, Whistle?" Whistle rests his snout on Coach's knees. "It's settled, then," Coach says.

Roselyn inches her way up. "I'd like to offer my services as a staffer for your rescue booth at Speedway." Her green eyes sparkle.

"Really?" I'm beyond excited—that's one of the key logistics we haven't figured out yet. "Are you sure you want to work at Speedway again?" I ask.

Roselyn nods. "I have Dr. Mac's Place to thank for giving me the courage to face my brother again. After your visit to the track, I called Manny. I told him he was doing the right thing and I wanted to help. Since then, things are much better between Manny and me." She gives all of us hugs.

Finally, Gran makes her way up front. She gives us bear hugs, too. Then, she raises her glass and says, "I'd like to make a toast." Dozens of glasses are raised in expectation. "A toast to Maggie and Taryn, and to the success of Gingerbread's Greyhound Rescue."

The melody of jingling, tinkling glasses and yipping, yapping dogs sounds even better than the racket of Ambler fans stomping their feet after I sink a winning shot!

Life in the Fast Lane

By J.J. MACKENZIE, D.V.M.

Wild World News—Everyone knows greyhounds are fast. They can run up to 45 miles per hour—almost as fast as a racehorse. The dogs' great speed eventually led to the modern sport of dog-track racing. But what most people don't know is that of all the many dog breeds around today, the greyhound is the oldest. The breed dates from the time of the ancient Egyptians.

Hark, Royal Hounds! Hounds are hunting dogs, and greyhounds are no exception. The Egyptians used greyhounds for hunting rabbit and gazelle as far back as 2500 BC. The dogs were such highly esteemed pets of royalty that they were mummified and buried with their owners. In ancient Arabia, the desert-dwelling Bedouins also kept greyhounds for hunting. Greyhounds were the only animals allowed inside their owners' desert tents, and some even got to ride with their owners on camelback.

In the Middle Ages and Renaissance, greyhounds were considered animals fit for royalty only. In England, it was illegal for commoners to keep a greyhound, and the punishment for breaking the law was death. Even after this law was changed, it was still quite a luxury for a commoner to obtain a greyhound for hunting.

Prairie Police to Racing Dogs. In the mid-1800s, greyhounds were imported to America in large numbers to rid pioneer farms of coyotes and jackrabbits. Farmers soon discovered that their speedy greyhounds could be used for sport. The first race, then called a *coursing meet,* was held in Kansas in 1886. Live rabbits were used as lures to attract the dogs and keep them running. The fences around the coursing area contained holes to allow some of the rabbits to escape. These coursing meets were rather chaotic events, with dogs and rabbits running every which way, and it wasn't always entirely clear which dog had won.

Around 1912, a man in California named Owen Patrick Smith invented the mechanical lure to address these problems. Smith's lure was a set of rabbit mannequins on a pole that moved in a large circle around a track. Using a lure instead of live rabbits made life easier for both the track owners and the rabbits! Smith's invention also allowed the greyhounds to run in a neat circle, making it much easier for the audience to watch the race and identify a winner.

A Dog's Life. Greyhound puppies are bred on breeding farms, where they spend much of their first six months in crates and kennels. After a year of training, they're given six chances to show strong racing ability. If they don't qualify, they are either put up for adoption or euthanized (put to death). Track racing is very hard on the dogs. Many suffer heart attacks and severely broken limbs. Some dogs are made to race even while injured. When they're not racing, the dogs spend most of their time in cramped cages, even though by nature greyhounds are as friendly and sociable as any other dog.

Even dogs with successful racing careers stop racing after age three of four, but they may live for another ten years—leaving their owners with the problem of what to do with retired racers.

Startling Statistics. The National Grey-

hound Assoc-
iation's records
show that each
year 38,000 new
greyhounds

**GREYHOUND RACING
IS POPULAR—BUT
IT IS NOT ALWAYS
PRETTY**

become racers, while approximately the
same number of older racing dogs retire.
Of these, 6,000 to 7,000 dogs get adopted
as pets. What happens to the other 31,000
dogs?

According to the Humane Society, every
year about 40,000 greyhounds in the United
States are either killed, sold to labs for
experimental research, or abandoned. These
unfortunate dogs include both retired racing dogs and young greyhounds who never
made it to the track.

Some dog owners care deeply about their
dogs and take good care of them, on and off
the track. Unfortunately, many do not. Since
the early 1980s, animal activists have been
working to expose racing's darker side and
to promote greyhound adoptions.

Turn the page to read a sample of the next book
in the Vet Volunteers series ...

New Beginnings

Chapter One

· · · · · · · · · · · ·

The tabby cat with black, gray, and white stripes is hanging out near the Dumpster behind our store again. I've seen him every day since we moved here a week ago. It's getting late and I promised Mom I'd help with dinner, but I want to see if the cat's okay. Yesterday, he had a tear in his left ear, but he was too jittery to let me look at it closely or to clean it.

"Hey there, kitty," I say. "How's your ear? Still no tags or collar?"

"Meow," he says. He watches me, but keeps his distance, his ring-striped tail twitching from side to side. Aside from no collar or tag, and his ear, which looks like it's healing okay, he doesn't look like a stray. His coat is short, thick, and shiny, and he looks well fed. In fact, he's more chubby than sleek. Each day he comes a little closer to me and the water dish I set out for him, and twice he's let me pet him. I've been changing the water daily. Maybe today he'll let me pet him again and check his ear more closely.

"Meow?" he says again, this time a question.

"Yes, you can trust me," I say.

He tilts his head, and his green eyes stare right at me.

My twin brother, Josh, says I have a sixth sense—Animal Sense.

"I won't hurt you."

The tabby is still skittish, but he's so cute. I love his markings—gray, black, and white stripes, with two thicker black lines in his fur on the top of head between his ears, forming what looks like a little M. He has more furry black V's accenting his eyes, and lots of fuzzy whiteness around his chin and neck. According to a cat website I found, he's a domestic shorthair brown mackerel tabby. But there is nothing common about him. His eyes and markings are so expressive. He's beautiful.

I kneel down a few feet behind the water dish and stay still. He finally approaches. He sniffs the water, laps at it, and then he walks closer to me.

I slowly lean forward, pausing before my hand reaches him. He sniffs it, and then rubs his furry forehead against my fingers. His slightly wet white whiskers tickle me as he tilts his head one way then another against my hand.

"Meow," he says again as I pet him, first his back, then his head, around his ears, including the ear with the little notch in it, and finally the warm, soft spot under his white chin until I feel and hear the vibration of his purr. Cats like me.

I miss petting the cats and kittens at the animal shelter back in Pittsburgh. This one reminds me of Moonshine, the orange tabby at the shelter. He was always a bit cautious, too. Before we moved here I volunteered there two days a week, helping clean up after the animals, washing their water and food dishes, petting and playing with the cats and kittens mostly, but sometimes the dogs and puppies, too. I helped get the animals socialized and friendly around people so they would have a better chance of being adopted.

"Where do you live?" I ask the tabby. "Do you have a home?"

He looks up at me as if he's about to tell me something important.

"Meow."

As soon as we get the hardware store Mom and

Dad bought all set up and open for business, I really want to volunteer at the shelter here in Ambler, too. I even got a recommendation letter from my supervisor back in Pittsburgh like Dad suggested. When the Ambler shelter sees my letter, I'm sure they'll let me volunteer.

The cat's purr gets louder and louder.

And I was excited to see that there's a veterinary clinic two blocks down the street. Maybe I'll make a copy of my letter to show the vets there, too. If I'm going to be a veterinarian someday, I have to get more experience, especially since we've never had any family pets of our own. Mom promised that we could finally get a pet once we'd settled in, but now she acts like it's the last thing on her mind.